PUFFIN BOOKS

TRIBES

Tribes is Catherine MacPhail's third children's book and was the winner of the Sheffield Award for Shorter Novels in 2002. Her previous books are *Run, Zan, Run,* which won the Kathleen Fidler Award and more recently the Verghereto Award in Italy, *Fighting Back,* which was awarded one of the first Scottish Children's Book Awards in 1999, and *Fugitive.* She also writes comedy, and has had two situation comedy series on Radio 2. Catherine lives in Greenock with her family, where she indulges her lifelong love of writing.

Other books by Catherine MacPhail

FIGHTING BACK
FUGITIVE

tribes

CATHERINE MACPHAIL

PUFFIN BOOKS

PUFFIN BOOKS

Published by the Penguin Group
Penguin Books Ltd, 80 Strand, London WC2R 0RL, England
Penguin Putnam Inc., 375 Hudson Street, New York, New York 10014, USA
Penguin Books Australia Ltd, 250 Camberwell Road, Camberwell, Victoria 3124, Australia
Penguin Books Canada Ltd, 10 Alcorn Avenue, Toronto, Ontario, Canada M4V 3B2
Penguin Books India (P) Ltd, 11 Community Centre, Panchsheel Park, New Delhi – 110 017, India
Penguin Books (NZ) Ltd, Cnr Rosedale and Airborne Roads, Albany, Auckland, New Zealand
Penguin Books (South Africa) (Pty) Ltd, 24 Sturdee Avenue, Rosebank 2196, South Africa

Penguin Books Ltd, Registered Offices: 80 Strand, London WC2R 0RL, England

www.penguin.com

First published 2001
10

Copyright © Catherine MacPhail, 2001
All rights reserved

The moral right of the author has been asserted

Set in 13/15 pt PostScript Monotype Baskerville
Typeset by Rowlands Phototypesetting Ltd, Bury St Edmunds, Suffolk
Printed and bound in England by Clays Ltd, St Ives plc

British Library Cataloguing in Publication Data
A CIP catalogue record for this book is available from the British Library

ISBN 0-141-30882-6

For my Sarah, my own little Glory

'*H*e must be here somewhere!'
    Kevin Davidson held his breath and pressed himself against the wall of the derelict shop. He tried to merge into the grey concrete, desperate to make himself invisible. Difficult when you're wearing a red tracksuit.

It didn't work.

'There he is!'

In the twilight, Kevin could just make out the boy with the black hair who was pointing at him. There was real venom in his voice. Why did he hate him? Kevin wondered. He had never seen him before, never seen any of them. Yet here they were, like a pack of rabid dogs drooling after him. Kevin threw himself forward and jumped over a broken wall. They broke into a run after him. One, two, three – more of them appearing from every direction.

'You can't run from us,' one of them shouted. 'You can't hide.'

They were right. He didn't know this part of town well enough to hide from them. Where could he go? Where was safe?

Nowhere. Not here. Not for him.

He kept running, though his legs were aching and

his heart was pounding. It was fear that kept him going.

Why were they after him? What had he ever done to them?

He had no doubt that this crowd meant to do some serious kicking if they caught him.

But why?

Because he was new in town?

They were closing in on him. He glanced behind and almost yelled when he saw how close they were. He rounded a corner and found himself heading for the car park underneath one of the tower blocks. Maybe he could hide himself there. Find a lift, an escape route. Someone to help him.

They were still behind him. He didn't dare look to see how near, but he could hear their feet pounding closer. If he didn't find a hiding place in this car park, he was done for.

Suddenly, one of them hooted, 'He's in here! We've got him now!' They were all screeching with delight at the thought of their prey, trapped. Then their chant began.

'We're the Rebels, and we always get our man!' Over and over.

Even in his terror, Kevin thought how stupid they sounded. He would have laughed another time. Everyone was in a gang around here. Kevin wasn't. He didn't belong to any of the gangs that roamed the area, battling with each other, preying on each other. Was that a reason to hate him? Maybe not. He was new in this part of town. Fair game.

'Keep away from those gangs, Kevin,' his dad had warned him when they moved here. But he'd hardly needed to be told. Kevin preferred his own company, or playing computer games with the one friend he had made so far – Tommy. Or going to the cinema. To join a gang, and belong, blend in with the others, that had never appealed to Kevin.

The darkness of the car park suddenly swallowed him up. His running footsteps echoed and the noises from the street seemed miles away now. Maybe, he thought, running in here hadn't been such a good idea after all.

He stopped for a second and looked around. There were always places to hide in films. Cars left open, keys handily left in the ignition so he could roar out past the Rebels and make his escape. He could almost picture their shocked, stupid expressions as he revved the car, gave them two fingers and raced off.

If someone had just been kind enough to leave their keys in the ignition, that is.

But no one would be stupid enough to leave a car door open in this area.

He slipped behind a pillar and tried to think. His eyes were growing accustomed to the darkness now and they zoomed around, searching for an escape. The green EXIT sign leapt at him. Wherever that door led to would be safer than where he was now.

'He has to be in here somewhere.' The voice was so close that Kevin caught his breath and was sure they had to hear him.

'We'll get him,' another voice said, 'and then he'll be sorry.'

Over my dead body, Kevin thought, and regretted thinking it at once. His dead body was probably what they had in mind.

He took a deep breath. He had to reach that door before they spotted him. He could make it, he was sure of that. Only one car stood between him and the EXIT door – and once he made it to that car he could crouch down behind it and move, unseen, to safety and freedom.

Crikey, he thought, I'm thinking like Arnold Schwarzenegger with a whole gang of killer robots behind him.

'Spread out!' a voice ordered. The leader. Kevin could tell by the authority in his tone.

The leader! What kind of boys were they who had to have a leader? Couldn't they think for themselves?

Well, not Kevin Davidson. He had brains, and he was going to use them to get out of here before this crazy bunch splattered them all over the concrete.

'You better get him!' The leader sounded angry, and that anger sent shivers up Kevin's spine.

Why was it so important to get him? One thirteen-year-old boy who had never done them any harm at all. Wasn't there some other poor idiot they could chase, harass, catch? What had he done to deserve their attention?

He looked again at the car, judging the distance. He could make it. He knew he could. He *was* going to get

4

away from them. He almost felt like thumbing his nose at them. He took one step, hidden by the pillar, into the darkness.

Go for it, Arnie baby, he thought to himself.

Another step, then another. Stealthy, like a panther. One more step and he would be completely hidden behind the car. Safe.

And that was when all hell broke loose.

The car's alarm began to screech. Its lights began to flash. Kevin looked behind him. They were all there, turning on him.

He was trapped. They were all around him, advancing. And all Kevin could do was to back up against the car that was still screeching out his presence like a traitor.

They were so close he could see their eyes, and there was hate, venom, viciousness in every pair. But why? This was so stupid. He didn't even know why they were after him.

The leader stepped forward. 'Let's show him what we do to people we don't like, boys,' he said.

Kevin took a deep breath. He wasn't going to go down without a fight. But it would be useless. There were too many of them. He was done for. Nothing could save him now.

2

Suddenly, a howling began from somewhere in the darkness close by. A howling like a wolf. It was a sound that sent shivers all through Kevin, setting the hairs on the back of his neck on edge.

The Rebels, advancing upon him, stopped. Kevin could see something in their eyes as they flicked from him to the blackness surrounding them. What was it? Apprehension? No. It was fear. Kevin tensed too. Was this another threat to him?

The howling came again, echoing eerily round the car park. One voice was all at once joined by many, a whole chorus of howling predators.

It had to be another gang, thought Kevin. Good. Let them knock holes out of each other. It might give him a chance to get away.

Then, without warning, the howling became a charging roar and through the blackness figures emerged, racing towards the Rebels. Black-jacketed figures, like panthers.

The Rebels turned from Kevin and they began roaring too. Heading straight towards the charging herd. Kevin was ready to make his move as soon as they did. He leapt for the EXIT door, but too late. Two boys fell against it, snarled up together, barring his way. Kevin stepped back. He was determined to keep out of it. It wasn't his battle. He just wanted away, to safety. Home.

The black jackets were getting the better of the Rebels. Kevin looked for another way out of the car park, a path through them. They'd never notice him going in the middle of all this.

Someone did. He was suddenly gripped by the throat and thrown to the ground. His head cracked against concrete.

'You did this!' Kevin recognized that voice. It was the leader of the Rebels.

But did what? What was he talking about?

The other boy was on him, his fist held in mid-air, ready to strike. 'You led us here, didn't you? You're one of them. This was an ambush.'

An ambush? This boy had been watching too many cowboy videos. Kevin would have told him that, but his mouth was too dry and all his attention was on that raised fist. That was why he didn't see the kick that sent his attacker flying off him with a cry of pain.

Kevin was on his feet in an instant, but so was the Rebel leader. His eyes were glittering with anger, or were they perhaps tears of pain? He glanced around to see who had kicked him. A small boy, much smaller than Kevin, made a run at the Rebel leader, but this time he was ready. He grabbed the boy, threw him to the ground and, as he lay there, lifted his foot, ready to smash it against the boy's head.

Kevin didn't even have to think about it. He hurled

himself forward, knocking the Rebel leader off his feet and to the ground. They rolled together and Kevin landed a punch on his face. He heard a satisfying yelp of pain, and the boy pushed him off and was on his feet once again.

The other Rebels had admitted defeat and had begun to run off. The leader had no choice. He was outnumbered. He backed away warily, his eyes never leaving Kevin. 'You watch your back, pal, 'cause we'll be after you.'

Then he was off, racing out of the car park along with the defeated Rebels. And that defeat would only feed more hate. Kevin stood up, watching after them. He jumped as a hand encircled his shoulders.

'Don't worry about him. That was MacAfee, and they're only the Rebels. They're nothing to be scared of.'

The voice was reassuringly soft. Kevin turned to see who it belonged to.

The boy wasn't any taller than Kevin, but there was a presence about him that made him look taller. His eyes were green, even in the half-light Kevin could see that. They reminded him of a cat's.

'I was blinkin' afraid of them,' he said.

The boy smiled. It was the kind of smile you couldn't help responding to. 'We saved you, didn't we?'

Kevin stopped smiling. He didn't like the idea of anyone saving him. Even if, in reality, they had. 'I would have got away from them eventually,' he said with a shrug.

'Yes . . . in a coffin.' The boy laughed and turned to his black-jacketed friends. 'Eh, boys?'

Kevin looked around at them as they all joined in the laughter. There were at least seven of them, including the small boy, who now stepped forward.

He punched Kevin on the shoulder. 'Thanks for helping me, mate. Saved me from a kicking. You're OK.'

'This is Torry,' the boy with the dark-green eyes said, ruffling the little boy's hair. 'And my name is Salom.'

Salom. The name rang a bell with Kevin. He had heard it, seen it. But where?

'And we are the Tribe.' He gestured round the rest of the gang with pride. 'Maybe you've heard of us?'

Hadn't everyone? Kevin thought. THE TRIBE RULES. He could see the graffiti on the walls all around the town.

'We're the best,' Torry told him, and there was a howl of agreement from the rest. Howling seemed to be one of the things the Tribe did better than anyone else.

'I'm Kevin.' He held out his hand and immediately felt stupid. It was such a grown-up, nerdy thing to do. But Salom grasped it and held it fast. He was still smiling.

'Nice to meet you, Kevin.'

'And thanks for . . .' He didn't know what he was thanking them for. He didn't actually believe they had saved him. They'd wanted a fight and had found an opportunity to have one. It was the Tribe who should be thanking him.

'I'd better be getting home,' he said.

'Ooo, will mummy be angry if you're late?' The voice was hostile. A tall ginger-haired boy came forward. His eyes were hostile too.

'Hey, Doc, leave Kev be. He helped Torry.' Salom patted his shoulder. 'He's a friend.'

'I'm fussy who I call my friend,' Doc said.

'This is Paul Docherty, Kevin. We call him Doc. He's not as friendly as the rest of us. But he's better on your side than against you, eh, Doc?'

'Yeah,' Doc said, still as unfriendly as before. 'Let him go home. He'll be safe now that they know he's one of us.'

Kevin snapped back. 'I'm not one of you. I'm not in a gang, and I don't ever want to be.'

Salom nudged him. 'Sure, Kev, don't listen to Doc. He talks too much.'

Kevin began to back out of the garage. They were all watching him – Torry giving him a friendly wave, Doc with something approaching hatred in his eyes.

And Salom.

It was hard to read what was in those smiling eyes. He stood straight, not the tallest of the group but the one your eyes were always drawn to.

Salom.

If only Kevin could remember where he had heard that name before.

3

*H*e got home to find his mother and father practising their line dancing in the living room. Line dancing was their hobby. No. It was their passion.

A passion? For line dancing? No wonder they embarrassed him. Their whole characters changed when they became line dancers. No more were they Mum and Dad. He became El Diablo, and his mother turned into Honey Sue. Embarrassing or what?

'Had a nice time, dear?' Honey Sue asked him breathlessly. She would have to lose some weight if she planned to keep this up, Kevin thought. He didn't tell her that, of course. Honey Sue would be liable to take off her ten-gallon hat and bash him with it.

Instead, he almost said to her, 'Oh yes, had a whale of a time. Been chased by one gang of psychopaths, and saved by another. Just another ordinary day in the life of Kevin Davidson.'

His father noticed Kevin was out of breath. 'You didn't have to run home, son.' He too was wearing a ten-gallon hat and his cowboy boots. Added to his beer-bottle glasses, it all made him look slightly ridiculous. El Diablo indeed! 'It's not as if you're late.'

'Kevin's never late,' Honey Sue said with a tender smile. 'We never have to worry about our Kevin.'

They didn't wait for him to tell them that maybe tonight they should worry. There was an intricate step they were trying to master and they turned all their attention on that.

The one in the family they *did* worry about was in the kitchen when Kevin went in there – his sister, Glory. She was bending across the ironing board with her hair spread all over it.

'What on earth are you doing, Glory?'

'I'm ironing my hair,' she said, as if it was the most natural thing in the world. Glory had a mane of long curly hair and she hated it. 'It makes it straight, it really does.' With that she stood up, took one long strand and held it out for Kevin to inspect. 'Straight as a die,' she said proudly. Then she let it go and it spiralled into a curl once again. Glory's face fell. 'It's not supposed to do that,' she said.

Kevin's eyes followed the flex of the iron. 'It might have worked if you'd plugged it in.'

Glory was only a year younger than Kevin and was always getting herself into bother about something or other. Not deliberately. There was nothing bad about Glory. But she was so naive that she walked into things anyone with any sense at all steered well clear of. Only recently she had wandered into Woolworths with a crowd from school who were known to indulge in a bit of shoplifting. Glory was the only one who didn't run fast enough when they were spotted. In fact, she didn't run at all. They all dumped what they had lifted on Glory as they raced past her, and Glory had calmly walked up to the store detective and handed it back.

Trouble was, she trusted people. She liked them. Not like Kevin. It took a lot before Kevin put his trust in anyone except himself.

Yet there were times when Glory was so sharp she could have cut hair. Now was one of those times.

'So, what were you running away from, Kev?'

He pushed shut the door of the kitchen on yet another doleful country and western dirge. 'A gang called the Rebels,' he told her.

'The Rebels,' Glory repeated thoughtfully. 'I've heard of them. "The Rebels Rule."' She emblazoned an imaginary slogan in the air. 'You see it all over the place.'

'Well, they didn't rule today.' Kevin began making himself a cheese sandwich. This getting chased certainly gave you an appetite. 'Today they were out-manoeuvred by the Tribe.'

'The Tribe?' Glory sounded impressed. 'You've met the Tribe?'

'They like to think they saved me,' he said.

'The Tribe saved you?' She was even more impressed. 'Wow! Are they letting you join them?'

'No, I am not joining them!' He bit into his sandwich. 'I don't join gangs. Certainly not one called the Tribe.'

'But they're the best,' Glory assured him. 'Everyone says so.'

For a moment Kevin thought about that. He had

been saved by the best. He remembered Salom and his dark-green eyes. Yes, he would only have the best in his gang. The image shimmered and was gone.

'I don't care if they've just won a Duke of Edinburgh Award. I don't intend joining any gang.'

'OK, don't get your Y-fronts in a twist,' Glory said. 'They probably wouldn't have a nerd like you anyway.'

He was almost insulted. Just then his dad appeared in the kitchen.

'What's all this about joining a gang?' he asked, eyeing Kevin's sandwich hungrily. 'Any more cheese?'

'I'm not joining any gang. Do you think I'm daft?'

'But if you did join a gang it would have to be the Tribe,' Glory said.

Did she never listen? Of course she never did.

'That's the one thing I want both of you to avoid. The gangs around here.' His dad spluttered bread and cheese over both of them. 'And Kevin will, he's far too sensible to want to be one of a crowd. He's unique. "To thine own self be true", Kevin, isn't that right?'

His dad looked at him fondly. He was always coming out with these sayings like 'The journey of a thousand miles begins with a single step' or 'Expect the best and only the best will come to you', always aiming them at Kevin, convinced they would never work on Glory. He looked at her now. 'And I don't want you joining any gangs either.'

Glory looked at him blankly. 'The only gang I'd

want to join is the Tribe, and they don't let girls in.'

'Who'd have her, anyway?' Kevin laughed. 'Except as a mascot.'

Later, as Kevin was going to bed, his dad spoke to him again, more seriously. 'I worry about Glory,' he said. 'She's so innocent.'

'She's stupid,' Kevin corrected him.

'She's naive, Kevin,' his dad insisted. 'Easily led. You'll let me know if she seems to be drawn to any of these gangs.'

'Like the Tribe,' he said, remembering her awe when she spoke about them. Yes, Glory was just the type to be sucked into a gang. 'I'll keep my eye on her, Dad.'

His dad smiled. 'Good lad. I never have any worries with you. I want you to know how much your mum and I appreciate that.'

Kevin went to bed that night feeling good. He liked making his parents happy. He wasn't a rebel like some of his friends. He wasn't into confrontation. Life was too short for that. Life was to be enjoyed with as little hassle as possible His sister was the only blot on his horizon. Dumb wasn't the word for her. She thought the Tribe was the best. So what? That didn't impress him, even if the graffiti all around the town proclaimed their superiority. Yes. Now he remembered seeing it everywhere.

THE TRIBE ARE TRIUMPHANT.
TRIBE ARE TOPS.

And in that second, just as he was drifting off to sleep, he remembered where he'd seen the name Salom. And that memory made him sit up, wide awake once more. He could see it now, a metre high, in black paint on the side of the old, derelict shops.

SALOM IS EVIL.

4

Over the next week, Kevin almost forgot about the Tribe. His days were spent with his pal, Tommy, at school. Their prime interest was in trying out for the school football team. His nights were spent in front of his computer, or Tommy's.

Then, one night as he walked home from Tommy's house, he heard a commotion behind the vacant lots. First, a scuffle that might have been a rat rummaging in the rubbish. Then a smash as if a bottle was being broken. His common sense told him to keep walking. No good would come of his sticking his nose in where it wasn't wanted. But when he heard a shout, a cry that could have been for help, he couldn't stop himself. His instinct was to hurry to where that noise was coming from.

There was a crowd of them. Boys, circled round one small boy with his back against the wall. Kevin could remember that feeling. He hadn't liked it one bit. He recognized the small boy at once. It would be hard not to. He was Torry. One of the Tribe.

Torry didn't looked scared at all. Small and wiry, he was swaying from side to side like a snake trying to hypnotize his victim. Someone, Kevin thought, should tell him he was supposed to be the victim here. There were three boys ranged against him, ready for a fight. Was that all they ever thought about? Fighting? A voice deep inside him urged him to go. Torry didn't need him. For all his size he looked as if he could take care of himself. The decision was taken out of Kevin's hands. Torry spotted him and there was a sudden moment of recognition, a flash of friendship. The three boys saw it at once. One of them turned on Kev. MacAfee, the leader of the Rebels. Kevin remembered his own brief encounter with him.

'He's one of them,' MacAfee said, not at all afraid. The odds were still in his favour, three against two.

But in the split second that their attention turned away from him, Torry took his chance. He leapt forward, catching them off guard, and downed two of them at once with a whoop of delight. Kevin had no choice but to tackle MacAfee. He ran at him, and the boy stumbled and lost his balance. He fell against the other two who were trying to get to their feet and they all toppled in a heap against some metal rubbish bins. The bins clattered noisily and their gooey, smelly contents spilled out. The three Rebels were mashed in the middle of half-eaten Chinese dinners and dirty nappies. Torry darted past them, grabbed Kevin by the arm and pulled him on.

''Mon,' he yelled. 'Before they get up.' Kevin took to his heels and ran with him. But Torry couldn't resist the temptation to shout back: 'You're rubbish, MacAfee, and that's just where you belong.' He grinned at Kevin. 'And we're the Tribe and you can never beat us!'

Even Kevin laughed. Torry was so delighted. And it hadn't been much of a fight. The other boys had been beaten easily.

They ran until they felt it was safe to stop, hidden in the maze of shops. 'You couldn't have come at a better time, Kev.' Torry's smile was infectious.

'Well, you couldn't have come at a better time for me the other night.'

Torry plunged his hands into his pockets and began walking beside Kevin.

'I'm not one of the Tribe, you know,' Kevin reminded him.

'You will be,' Torry said, as if he knew something Kevin didn't. 'Soon as you pass the initiation test.'

Kevin stopped walking. 'What initiation test?'

Torry laughed. 'You don't just walk into the Tribe, pal,' he said. 'First you've got to pass the test.'

'I told you. I don't want in.' The plain truth. Why didn't anyone believe him?

'You will,' Torry said. 'We took a vote. Everyone's for it.' Then he shrugged. 'Except for Doc. He doesn't seem to like you much. But the rest of us do. You're OK. You've proved it. You're a good fighter, and you helped me tonight.' Torry slapped him on the back. 'I'll tell Salom. He likes you.'

SALOM IS EVIL. It all came back to him in that moment, just as Torry began to run off.

'Salom will be in touch,' Torry shouted. 'Pass the test . . . and you're one of us, officially.'

Then he was gone, his running footsteps echoing on the wet pavements.

'I don't want to be one of the Tribe,' Kevin shouted after him. But he was long gone, and Kevin's voice was heard by no one except stray cats.

If this Salom sought him out, he would tell him he wasn't interested in joining any gang. And he certainly wasn't going to put himself through any initiation test.

Yet he was curious. What kind of test was it? It sounded painful, and he didn't approve of pain. Especially his own.

SALOM IS EVIL.

The words scared him. Who had written them, and why?

It seemed to Kevin, as he walked home that night, that it would be much better to steer well clear of the Tribe, and of this boy called Salom.

Unfortunately, Salom didn't steer well clear of Kevin.

5

'*A*re you sure you're not a member of the Tribe?' Glory asked him a few days later.

This was getting to be too much. Everyone was asking him the same thing. It had gone all round the school and he had noticed a little touch of awe from some of the more stupid pupils. Even Tommy, his pal Tommy who should have known better, had asked him and hadn't been reassured by his answer.

'It's just that everybody's talking about it, Kev,' he had said. 'You would tell me if you'd joined? I mean, you wouldn't be sworn to secrecy or anything, would you?'

'I'd tell the world,' Kevin said, 'even if I'd been sworn to secrecy under pain of death.'

Now even his sister wouldn't let it go.

'Do you think I suffer from memory loss?' he snapped at her. 'No! No! And no again!' She seemed disappointed. 'Do you think I'm daft enough to go through an initiation test?'

The fact that he wasn't seemed to disappoint her even more.

'They say the Tribe's initiation test is the most . . .' She tried to find the right word to describe it but couldn't.

Kevin tried to help her. 'Scary?'

She shook her head. 'No, the Rebels' is scary. You have to stay overnight in the cemetery. Big deal. Every drunk in the town does that.'

'Risky?' Kevin suggested.

'No. The Knights' is risky. You have to shoplift and if you're caught you just don't get in.'

'Well, you might get into a young offenders' institution, of course.' He couldn't imagine anyone being so stupid as to risk their freedom just to get into a daft gang. 'Dangerous then,' he said.

Glory thought about that. Now, how did his dizzy sister know so much about these initiation tests? That amazed him. Dad was right. He would have to watch out for her.

Suddenly, Glory's eyes went wide. 'No, not so much dangerous as terrifying.'

'So, what is it then?' he asked her.

'No one knows. They're sworn to secrecy after they join. And not one of the Tribe has ever broken that solemn oath. So nobody knows what the initiation test is.' She sounded even more impressed. 'That's why the Tribe is the best.'

'So all these —' now he tried to think of the right word to describe the members of the Tribe — 'all these sheep,' he decided, 'never tell. And you think that's wonderful, do you?'

'Not just me,' she said defensively. 'Everybody does.'

Kevin laughed. 'Well, I tell you what, Glory. Just

for you, I'll join the Tribe, find out what their secret initiation test is, and I'll tell the world.'

And he would. He'd tell everyone. He'd never heard anything so stupid as all this secrecy and sacred oaths.

Yet he couldn't escape talk of the Tribe. It was everywhere, and he was always included in it, as if he was already one of them.

Mr Lever at the paper shop warned him not to get involved. 'I don't intend to,' Kevin told him.

Mr Lever liked Kevin. He was dependable and trustworthy, not like a lot of the boys around his area. 'It was just that I heard a rumour that you'd joined one of them.'

'I know, I've heard it too. But I haven't and I won't.'

Mr Lever seemed satisfied. 'I'm glad. That Salom boy is a real bad lot.'

SALOM IS EVIL.

Yet the picture that came up in Kevin's mind was of a smiling, pleasant boy.

'Why is he a bad lot?' Kevin asked.

Mr Lever shrugged. 'Don't know much about him. Caused some bad trouble where he lives. Just you keep away from him.'

Mr Lever really didn't have an answer. Salom was as mysterious as ever.

Yet there seemed to be no mystery about the boy who waited for Kevin as he hurried home from school next day.

Salom was sitting on a wall, and he smiled engagingly when Kevin appeared.

'Hi, Kev,' he said, jumping from the wall and falling into step beside him. 'I came to thank you for helping Torry.'

'I didn't actually do very much. I was just at the right place at the right time.'

'Thanks anyway. Torry, he's one of the best,' Salom said. 'But the scrapes he gets into!' With that he laughed and slapped Kevin on the back. Kevin laughed too. It was hard not to.

Salom went on. 'He's caused us more problems than he's worth.' Then he added, 'No, I take that back. We wouldn't be the same without Torry. He's special.'

Kevin liked that; liked how he stuck up for Torry.

'We?' Kevin asked, though he knew the answer. 'Who're we?'

Salom shrugged. 'The Tribe, of course.'

'I can't get away from the Tribe. That's all I hear about.'

'Tribes are Tops,' Salom said. Then he laughed so heartily Kevin couldn't help but join in. 'I know what you're thinking. It's crazy. Gangs. I felt the same. But everyone round here is in one. It's just like a club.'

'Like the Boy Scouts?' Kevin suggested.

That made Salom laugh even harder. 'We just have more fun.'

'And more fights,' said Kevin.

Salom didn't agree with that. 'We try to keep away from fights. But it's hard. We have this reputation, see?'

'You're the best?' Kevin said.

Salom smiled. 'Of course we are. We don't need to fight to prove it. But the others, they're always after us, especially the Rebels. They want to be the best, and if they beat us . . .'

He left it hanging in the air, the idea that if the Rebels could beat the Tribe, the Rebels would take over as the best.

They walked on for a while in silence. It was only as they reached Kevin's corner that Salom spoke again. 'I wish you'd join.'

'Why?' Kevin wanted to know. Because if they were the best, so exclusive, why should they need him?

'Because I think we'd all have good fun.'

Good fun? Somehow fun was something Kevin had never associated with the gangs.

'Everyone likes you,' Salom said.

Kevin remembered the boy with the red hair and the hostile eyes. 'Doc didn't.'

'Doc doesn't like anybody. It's just his way. He's all right when you get to know him.'

'You're the leader,' Kevin said. 'I don't want anyone to be my leader.'

Salom laughed again. 'Silly, isn't it? But it's just a title. Everyone gets a turn. We vote on it.'

Salom thought it was silly too. That surprised Kevin. And it kind of pleased him.

'And I most certainly wouldn't go through any mysterious initiation test just to join.'

'No?' Salom sounded surprised now. 'I didn't think you'd be scared of anything.'

For a minute that made Kevin bristle with pride. 'What is this initiation test anyway?'

Salom shook his head. 'Oh no, I've sworn not to tell. Sorry. I'm just like the rest of the Tribe when it comes to this.'

'Sworn to secrecy!' Kevin said dramatically.

Salom smiled that slow smile of his. 'Sworn to secrecy!' he said in exactly the same tone.

Kevin decided right then that he liked Salom. He couldn't help himself. But joining the Tribe? Going through some terrifying test? Being sworn to secrecy? That wasn't for him. It was stupid.

He thought about what he'd said to his sister. That he would join just to find out what the test was and then he would tell everybody. That would prove once and for all that he wasn't one of the sheep.

First, though, he would have to pretend he wanted to join the Tribe.

He thought about all this as he looked into Salom's smiling eyes. Somehow he felt that Salom knew what he was thinking and agreed with him.

It was that feeling which made him decide. 'OK,' he said. 'I'll give it a try. I will join the Tribe.'

6

'We're performing our line dancing in the shopping mall on Saturday,' Dad told them proudly as they sat down to breakfast next morning.

Kevin choked on his cornflakes. 'What? Do you mean in front of people?'

'Of course,' his mother said, entertaining them with a little step as she made the coffee. 'It's for charity.'

Even Glory was mortified. 'Oh, Mum! What if any of my friends see you?'

'Just tell them to pop their donation in the bucket like everyone else.'

His dad laughed. There was a time when such a thought would have embarrassed him too. Then line dancing had come into their lives like a disease. Kevin was sure his parents hadn't always been this crazy.

Glory was almost crying. 'My friends are more likely to vomit in the bucket than anything else.'

Kevin went to school depressed. His mum and dad intended to make complete fools of themselves in the town centre on Saturday. And he was due to meet the Tribe tonight after his paper round. Tonight he would undergo the secret initiation test. He didn't believe for a minute it would be as terrifying as everyone thought. It was more likely to be just plain embarrassing. He was going to make as big a fool of himself as his mum and dad would on Saturday.

At the bus stop he met Tommy and told him all about the line dancing.

'Just come to the pictures tonight with me. That'll cheer you up,' Tommy said when he'd finished laughing.

Kevin almost said 'yes'. Then he remembered he had other plans. He told Tommy all about them too.

'Why did you ever say you would join?' Tommy asked. Like Kevin, he thought the gangs were stupid.

Kevin wished he knew the answer. His original reason, to find out what this test was, seemed crazy now.

'Are you scared?' Tommy asked.

'No,' Kevin said, and it was true. The very idea of an initiation test was laughable. He had heard of so many. 'I mean, what are they going to make me do? Slip a grass snake down the front of my trousers?' The thought made him squirm, but he could handle it.

Tommy's suggestion was worse. 'Maybe they'll make you eat worms. Imagine them wriggling about in your mouth.' Both boys did, and almost spewed up in the street.

'Perhaps if I tell them I'm a vegetarian, they'll let me eat something else instead.'

Just then, they noticed a dog doing its business on the pavement in front of them. Kevin looked at Tommy. They both turned green. Kevin shook his head. 'No, I think I'd probably prefer the worms.'

'Just what is it that makes the Tribe's initiation test so secret?' Tommy wondered. 'Why won't anyone tell?'

'I'll tell,' Kevin said with decision. 'I promise. By this time tomorrow everyone is going to know the Tribe's secret. And they won't be so special any more.'

'And if they're not, none of the other gangs will be either.' Tommy patted his pal on the back. 'Good on you, Kevin. I think it's a great idea.'

The Tribe were waiting for him at the old harbour. Well, three of them anyway – Torry balancing on one of the old capstans, Doc standing with his arms folded, face grim, by the harbour wall and Salom standing silhouetted against the golden river set on fire by the evening sun.

'Where are the rest of the Tribe?' Kevin asked, looking around for them.

'Call us the initiation test committee.' Salom laughed. 'Ready, sport?' he asked him.

'Ready for anything?' Torry laughed.

'What do you mean, anything?' Kevin felt his stomach sink. Now it was so close, he was apprehensive. 'What exactly is this initiation test?'

'You'll see,' said Salom.

'I still don't trust him.' This was Doc, hostile as ever.

Torry advanced and pulled on Kevin's arm. 'Come on, let's go.'

'Let's go where?' Kevin asked. But they wouldn't

tell him. In fact, all the way, they wouldn't talk to him at all. And that was what really began to scare Kevin.

They took the bus along the road that bordered the river, to the far end of town. From there, they walked past the cinema and to the top of the hill, heading towards the old disused whisky warehouse that stood dominating the skyline of the town.

It was an ugly old building, red brick, with every window smashed and half the inside missing. At night, whenever Kevin would pass those broken windows, they reminded him of sunken skeleton eyes. Now, as they approached it in the twilight, it looked even scarier. He had often imagined how terrifying it would be to be trapped in there in the dark. Now, with a shudder, he had a feeling that was going to be his fate.

'Is that where we're going?' he asked.

Salom grinned. 'That's where we're going.'

Kevin felt his pulse quicken and his heart began to beat faster. He had a notion to run then but, at that moment, Salom slipped an arm around his shoulder, friendly, yet very firm, leading him inside the gaping mouth of that redbrick monster.

'Come, my friend,' he said. 'There's no turning back now.'

It was really dark inside the building, but Kevin wasn't given a chance for his eyes to become accustomed to the blackness. Doc pulled a scarf from his jacket pocket.

'What are you going to do with that?' Kevin asked him.

'Blindfold you,' Doc said stonily.

'What? Are you not going to let me see what I'm doing?'

Maybe they *were* going to make him eat something awful, then guess what it was.

Doc tied the blindfold roughly round his eyes. This boy didn't like Kevin, that was for sure.

'If you're going to tie me up here all night,' Kevin said, trying to sound as if the thought didn't bother him at all, 'someone will have to tell my parents I'm staying over with them.'

Again it was Doc who answered sarcastically. 'You think it's going to be that simple? Stay the night in the old dark warehouse?'

'That's kids' stuff,' Torry said.

'You'll soon know what it is, Kev,' Salom said, at the same time guiding him gently. 'Be careful. We're going up the stairs.'

Going up. That phrase scared him too. Kevin was scared of heights, always had been. He could visualize the stairs in this old building. Broken, crumbling, dangerous. And he was going up them, blindfolded. This had to be the daftest thing he'd ever done.

Step by faltering step he climbed, held gently but firmly by Salom, who encouraged him in his soft voice. 'One more step here, Kev. Now we're turning. Almost there.'

Sometimes a hand would push him roughly forward. He knew who that belonged to – Doc, pushing him so hard he almost tripped.

And he could hear Torry skipping up the stairs behind him, laughing. Looking forward to what was ahead.

What was ahead? How high were they going? It seemed to Kevin that they had been climbing for ever.

He was breathing hard. But it wasn't from the climb. He knew that. It was nerves.

He had never been inside this building and could only imagine how it looked. Did these stairs lead anywhere? Did they plan to abandon him here, blindfolded? Or did they intend to lead him to a broken wall, then push him over? He could imagine Doc doing that with glee. He could even imagine Torry whooping with laughter as he did. But, with Salom at his elbow, he felt reassured. Salom wouldn't do that to him.

But where was he going?

He could hear faint traffic noises far below.

Far below.

How far?

He tried to remember how many storeys this warehouse had. Seven? Eight? He'd never counted, in all the times he'd passed here and looked up. Now he wished he had.

They came to a final step and, as Salom turned him on to a landing, Kevin felt a gust of cold night air from a broken window.

'We're here,' Salom said, turning Kevin towards him. 'Doc, take off the blindfold.'

As roughly as he had put it on, Doc whipped it off.

Kevin blinked. It took a few seconds for his eyes to grow accustomed to the darkness. And it was dark now. No moon. No stars. A cloudy sky overhead.

He looked around him. They were high in the building, not quite on the top floor, but near enough. Dust and broken glass lay everywhere. Behind him, the crumbling stairs he had just climbed. In front of him . . .

Kevin gasped and stepped back. In front of him was nothing. He was standing at the edge of a gaping chasm, a hole that stretched to nothingness below. At the other side of that chasm, it looked a million miles away, was a minute stretch of floor and a smashed window. And all that connected the floor Kevin was standing on to that other side was a narrow wooden beam. Kevin looked at Torry. He was smiling, his hands on his hips. He looked at Doc. There was something malevolent in his eyes. And then he looked at Salom. He stepped on to the beam like an acrobat. Kevin gasped.

Salom grinned. 'You get to the other side, and you are a fully paid-up member of the Tribe.'

They couldn't be serious. They expected him to cross over there. Below him, a sheer drop? No way!

Salom stepped back and gestured to the beam, like a magician. 'Welcome,' he said, 'to the Walk of Death.'

7

*K*evin took a step back; he couldn't help himself. Doc's hand on his back pushed him forward again.

'Scared?' he asked, his voice full of sarcasm.

Torry swaggered on the edge. 'Come on, Kev. You can do it. Even I've managed it.' Then he laughed. 'But I'll never be crazy enough to do it again.'

Kevin felt his mouth go dry. He tried to swallow, but couldn't. He tried not to look down, but it was impossible.

Down, and down, and down. Floor by broken floor. He imagined himself falling, arms flailing wildly, his jacket billowing behind him. What would he be thinking about as he fell?

How the heck had he ever got himself into this?

He was shaking now, and Doc, his hand still pressed against Kevin's back, could feel it. 'Told you this one was a wimp, Salom,' he said viciously. 'He's shaking like a baby.'

They laughed, Torry and Doc; but not Salom.

Salom only looked. It was a look that seemed to say, 'You can do it, Kevin. Don't let me down.'

Kevin found his voice at last. 'What would happen if I said I just didn't want to do it?'

Salom shrugged. 'It's never happened. The people we ask to join the Tribe are special. Afraid of nothing.'

Salom didn't expect him to say no. And Kevin suddenly knew he had no intention of not doing it.

He was going to attempt the Walk of Death.

The realization made him shake even more. 'Has anyone ever fallen?' he asked breathlessly.

For a long time, it seemed to Kevin, no one answered him.

'Of course not,' Salom said at last.

'Are you going to start or aren't you?' Doc pushed him forward again. Kevin's foot kicked at some rubble, and debris spilled over the edge of the hole, tumbling into the blackness far below.

'If you don't hurry up, I'll need a Zimmer to get out of here.' Torry gave him a friendly nudge. 'Go on, Kevin. It'll be over in five minutes.'

And I might be all over too, Kevin thought, all over the place. Splat!

Kevin drew in a long breath. He stood up straight. Doc took his hand away from his back. Even Torry was still.

'When . . . when I get to the other side . . . do I have to walk back?' His voice was shaking. He couldn't stop it.

'No fear!' Salom said. 'There's a fire escape outside that window. Stairs down to the next floor.'

'You only have to walk across, it's not far,' Doc said in a sing-song voice, as if Kevin were a little boy.

Salom said encouragingly, 'Don't look down,

34

Kevin. Pretend you're only two metres off the ground. You'd dance along the beam then, wouldn't you? You wouldn't even think of falling.'

Sure I would, Kevin thought, because I'd know that if I fell I wouldn't hurt myself.

But he said nothing. He was going to need all his concentration. Salom was right. If he was going to make it, he'd have to forget that long, long drop.

He could hear his father's voice. 'The journey of a million miles begins with a single step,' he would say. I'm beginning, Dad, he thought and he took one nervous step on to the beam. He looked across to the other side. Safety. In five minutes it would be all over. He held on to that thought and took one more step.

It was as if every sound in the world stopped and all that was left was the beating of Kevin's heart. Thump. Thump. Thump.

Salom's voice came softly from behind him. 'We'll treat you to fish and chips after this, Kev,' he said. 'Celebration meal.'

Fish and chips. Something else to look forward to. And safety.

One more step.

For a split second he was aware that he was suspended above that black hole. He shoved the thought away. Mustn't think about that. Too scary.

Another step.

He had to keep his mind off what was below him. Nothing.

I'll tell the whole town, the whole world, about the

Walk of Death when I'm finished, he said to himself. It won't be a secret any more.

Wait till I tell Tommy what I've done. He really will think I'm crazy.

And another step.

He was in the middle.

Nothingness all around him.

Nothing to cling on to.

Nothing to reach for.

Nothing.

No!

Mustn't think about that.

I can't do this, he thought. And again, his dad's voice floated into his mind. 'You can if you think you can, and if you think you can't you're probably right.'

I can. I can. He kept repeating that over and over. I can.

He had no choice now, anyway. Going back was as dangerous as going on. He had to get to the other side.

One more step.

Salom's voice came softly again. 'You're almost there, Kevin.'

Almost there. Hang on to that, Kevin son, almost there.

He imagined Torry smiling behind him, willing him to make it. Had he run across when it had been his turn?

Suddenly, he could picture Doc. If he was to yell out now or clap his hands, Kevin would lose his footing. Doc didn't like him.

One more . . .

His foot didn't quite hit the beam squarely. It slipped. Torry gasped. Kevin swayed, tried to hold his balance. I can. I can. I can . . .

He placed his foot firmly on the beam.

'Good boy!' Salom whispered.

Another step.

He would make it. He could almost smell the fish and chips.

And another.

Safety was only three steps away.

It was at that moment that a soft chorus began. Salom's voice first, joined by Torry and then Doc.

The Tribe. The Tribe. The Tribe.

The rhythm of the chant urged him forward.

The Tribe. The Tribe. The Tribe.

He took another step with assurance. Then another.

With the last he leapt to firm, safe ground.

He had made it! He had done it! He had walked the Walk of Death and lived!

He looked across the chasm at Torry and Doc and Salom. All chanting.

The Tribe! The Tribe! The Tribe!

And suddenly all three boys lifted their faces to the sky and began to howl.

Something ancient and tribal rose in Kevin too. And he howled as joyously and loudly as the rest of them.

8

'So, how do you feel now?' Salom handed him his fish and chips, as if it was an award for bravery.

Kevin thought for a minute. How did he feel?

Exhausted. Yes. Drained. Definitely. Yet his whole body tingled with exhilaration. Now it was over, all he could remember was the thrill, the excitement.

Even the memory of the fear excited him.

'I feel brilliant,' he said, and he wasn't lying. He felt alive, really alive for the first time in his life.

Salom smiled broadly. 'I knew you'd feel like that. We all did. It's the best feeling in the world.'

Kevin began to eat his fish and chips. He hadn't realized he was this hungry. 'That Walk of Death fairly gives you an appetite,' he said with a grin.

Salom watched him with amusement.

'What's so funny?' Kevin asked.

'You can't tell now, can you?'

Kevin didn't answer for a moment. Then he said, 'How did you know?'

Salom dipped into Kevin's chips. 'Because I was going to do the same thing. Tell everyone. Thought it was stupid. Just like you. Then I did the Walk of Death . . . and I knew I couldn't tell anyone.'

And neither could Kevin. Right or wrong, he was

one of the Tribe now. And the thought made him feel good.

Salom's grin grew wider. He slapped Kevin on the back. 'Now we're like brothers. Best friends. We'll always be there for each other. No matter what. Right?'

Kevin nodded.

Torry bounced out of the chip shop balancing a chip on his nose. 'This was like you, Kevin, up there.' The chip wavered and fell, but Torry caught it deftly and popped it in his mouth. 'See, when you were halfway across there and you almost fell . . .' Torry rolled his eyes in terror and he let out a howl. A Tribe howl.

The people around the door of the chip shop and waiting in the queue recognized it and watched them warily.

What was the feeling Kevin suddenly had? It took him only a second to know. It was pride. Pride that he was one of them.

What was happening to him? Why had his feelings changed so suddenly?

He knew the answer to that without thinking.

He had walked the Walk of Death. So had Torry and Doc. So had Salom and the other members of the Tribe. Only them.

They were special.

Doc came out of the chip shop and joined them. He still didn't smile. There was still an unfriendly look in his eyes. But what he did then was worth more than a smile. He held out his hand. 'You did good,' he said.

'Good?' Salom shouted. 'The boy did brilliant!'

And suddenly he was howling. They were all howling and running and laughing and throwing chips at each other.

Later, Salom went striding off with a jubilant Torry, and Kevin was left with Doc to walk the last few blocks home. Then he remembered something that had been bothering him. It had been bothering him since those terrifying, exciting moments just before he stepped on to the Walk of Death.

'I asked a question before, Doc,' he said, 'and it took a long time for me to get an answer.'

Doc didn't even look at him. He kept on walking, his hands sunk deep into his pockets.

Kevin pulled him back by the elbow and Doc turned to face him.

'I asked if anyone had fallen before,' Kevin said. 'Someone did, didn't they?'

Doc stared at him for a moment, considering his answer. 'We don't know what happened. No one does.'

'Who?' Kevin asked.

'Stash,' Doc said at once. 'He was my best pal. They said he'd been playing in the old warehouse and must have fallen through one of the floors.' Doc shrugged. 'Could have been, I suppose.'

'But you don't think so?' Kev had a feeling Doc wasn't telling him everything.

Doc shook his head. 'He'd already done the Walk of Death. Who'd be crazy enough to try it again?'

Then Doc was off, running away from him. Running away from any more difficult questions.

Stash? thought Kevin. Who was Stash? And why had he tried the Walk of Death again?

9

Glory was still up when he got home. El Diablo and Honey Sue could be clearly heard practising in their bedroom. Lucky, thought Kevin, they lived in a bottom flat.

Glory, her hair tied up in a ponytail, was sitting cross-legged on his bed, chewing gum and wearing his best Manchester United top as her pyjamas.

'Get that off right now!' he shouted. The euphoria brought on by the Walk of Death was gone in an instant.

'But it was in the wash. I didn't think you'd mind,' she said, blowing a bubble.

'Well, I do. Get it off.'

She shook her ponytail petulantly. Kevin's eyes widened in horror. 'What is that holding up your ponytail, Glory?'

She looked puzzled, but he didn't wait for her answer.

'Is that a pair of your knickers?'

She giggled. 'Of course. I can't find my bobble.' She said it as if it was the most natural thing in the world to wrap your knickers round your hair!

'You embarrass me! If you ever do that when any of my friends are here, you're dead, Glory!'

Glory was unbelievable. 'You are so boring, Kevin.' She made a face and disappeared.

Unfortunately, not for long. She was back a few minutes later, this time wearing one of Dad's old shirts. It drowned her.

'Haven't you got any pyjamas of your own?'

'Course. But it's all baby stuff. I look stupid in them.' Kevin looked her up and down. The shirt hung below her knees and the sleeves dangled well beyond her hands. 'And you don't think you look stupid now?' he asked her.

She ignored that and threw herself down on his bed. 'Where were you?' she asked.

'None of your business,' he replied.

'Are you a member of the Tribe now? Did you meet Salom tonight? What was the initiation test like?'

'None of your business. None of your business . . . and . . .' He pretended to think. 'What was the last question again? Oh yes. None of your business.'

She looked genuinely disappointed, and surprised. 'But you said you would tell me.'

And he had. It seemed an age away now. In another time zone. A time before the Walk of Death. 'Get to bed, Glory. I'm tired.'

She stood up and flapped one of Dad's long sleeves at him. 'I waited up specially,' she said with a pout. 'What made you change your mind?'

'I haven't,' he lied, deciding it was easier than telling the truth. 'I'm just too tired. It was all that wrestling with the boa constrictor down at the zoo.'

Glory's eyes went wide. 'You didn't! Was that the initiation test?' Then her eyes narrowed. 'Are you kidding me on, Kev?'

He pretended to be hurt. 'Me? Kid on my clever little sister? Never!'

'I'll find out. You see if I don't!'

Glory had a habit of finding out all sorts of useless gossip. Kevin was confident she'd never find out this.

She stood at the bedroom door. 'Did you at least find out what happened to Stash?'

The question shocked him. He'd never heard of Stash before tonight, yet his slightly stupid little sister seemed to know all about him.

'What about Stash?'

Glory shrugged her shoulders and Dad's shirt almost fell off her. 'It happened before we moved here. He was one of the Tribe and he died, fell or something.' She paused, watching for his reaction. 'Some people think he was pushed.'

That shocked him even more. Stash pushed from the Walk of Death? But who would push him?

Tommy was waiting for him next morning at the end of the street, anxious to know everything. 'OK, what

43

happened? Did you meet them? Did you do the initiation test? What was it?' His questions poured out.

What was he going to tell him? He had promised to reveal all. But he couldn't ever do that now. Not even to Tommy. 'I didn't meet them,' he lied. It had taken him a long time to answer and he was sure Tommy didn't believe him. 'They didn't turn up.'

Tommy looked puzzled, but after a moment he only shrugged. 'Just as well. Better not get involved at all, eh?'

Kevin swallowed. He hated lying. Especially hated lying to Tommy. 'Yeah,' he said, as if it didn't matter to him either.

They walked on for a while in silence.

'Remember tonight?' Tommy said as they neared the school gates. 'You promised to come with me to the dentist after school. I'll never have the nerve to go by myself.'

'Coward!' Kevin teased, laughing and chasing him down the street.

He wasn't a coward. The thought hit him immediately. He had walked the Walk of Death. The dentist would never hold any fears for him again.

It was there in the back of his mind all day. As he went through all the motions of an ordinary school day, one thought kept surfacing – the Walk of Death. He relived it again and again. The feelings he had had, the fear, the terror, the exhilaration.

He would look around at his classmates and wonder what they had done last night. Football practice? Some television? But nothing as exciting as what he had done. It made him feel different, superior. He couldn't help it. He was one of the Tribe.

'What's wrong with you?' Tommy asked him at lunchtime. 'You're in a dream.'

Kevin could only answer, 'Can't be bothered being at school. What do you think?'

Salom was waiting for him as he came out of the school gates with Tommy close at his heels. He smiled broadly but his smile, Kevin noticed, didn't include Tommy.

'Hi, Kev!' he called, jumping to his feet and slipping an arm round his shoulders. 'We've got to hurry. The rest of the Tribe are waiting.'

'Waiting? Waiting for what?'

'You'll see,' Salom said. He began to walk off with Kevin beside him. At the last moment, Kevin remembered Tommy, still trying to keep up with him. He turned and waved.

'Bye, Tommy, I've got to go, but I'll see you tomorrow, eh?'

It was only later, much later, he remembered his promise to go with him to the dentist.

10

Salom led Kevin behind one of the derelict shops in the old shopping precinct.

They walked up an alley scattered with papers and broken bottles. Doors were covered with metal to stop vandals from getting inside, but they had reckoned without the ingenuity of the gangs around here. Or one of them, the Tribe.

'I hope they never knock these old shops down,' Salom said. 'This is our place.' And with that he swung one of the metal doors across and stepped inside.

They were all waiting. Tonight, all of the Tribe were there. Standing, sitting, crouching on upturned boxes, or on old chairs. The shop wasn't dark. It was lit by the eerie glow from candles, which were placed all around the shop floor.

It reminded Kevin of church.

'What are we here for?' For one awful moment he thought that yet another initiation test was involved.

'The oath of allegiance, what else?' Salom said.

Kevin laughed. 'Aw, come on, you're not serious. You expect me to take an oath?'

'It's nothing,' Salom assured him. 'It's the final ritual, then you really *are* one of us.'

This was stupid. Kevin knew it was stupid. But he

said nothing. He let them gather around him, there in the candlelight.

'So, what do I say?' he asked at last.

Salom's voice was solemn. He took a scroll, covered with dark stains, from his inside pocket and began reading. 'Repeat after me. I, Kevin Davidson . . .'

'I, Kevin Davidson . . .'

'Do solemnly swear . . .'

'Do solemnly swear . . .'

'To be a true and faithful member of the Tribe.'

Kevin repeated everything after Salom. Part of him wanted to laugh, but there was also a part that was impressed: by the atmosphere, by the candlelight, by the serious faces all around him.

'I will never disclose any of the Tribe's secrets, I will never betray another member of the Tribe and, if I do, may my heart be ripped out and I be haunted for the rest of my life by ghosts and demons.'

'Is that it?' Kevin said when he had finished.

'No.' Doc stepped from the gloom in a far corner. 'Now you sign it in blood.'

Kevin hesitated. '*My* blood?'

'Well, it better not be mine!' This was Torry, and it made everyone in the dark shop laugh.

Except Kevin. He didn't like the idea of this 'blood' at all.

'We've all done it,' Salom reassured him, 'and lived to tell the tale.'

Except Stash . . .

Suddenly, Salom produced a knife from his pocket.

47

Kevin took a step back. But Doc was there behind him. 'Don't be scared, Kevy-boy. One little nip and it'll all be over.'

Doc grabbed his hand and held it out. Kevin struggled. Salom looked into his eyes.

'I'm only going to cut your palm and let the blood drip on this.' *This* was the scroll he had been reading from. Now Kevin understood the stains. They were blood too. The blood of every other member of the Tribe.

Kevin held his breath. He had walked the Walk of Death. One little cut would be nothing to him.

He tensed as Salom came closer, and the blade of the knife gleamed in the candlelight. Kevin closed his eyes.

Pain seared into him as the knife cut into his flesh. Only then did he open his eyes. Salom held the scroll under his hand and Kevin watched as the blood dripped, drop by drop, on to the paper. And then, in the gloom, the chant began again, more eerie this time.

The Tribe . . . The Tribe . . . The Tribe . . .

And finally, the howl. Even Kevin howled.

Suddenly, Torry yelled at the top of his voice, 'Let's *party*!'

And they did. Music erupted from someone's radio. They danced and they jumped and they sang. They told crazy jokes, and Kevin laughed so much he thought his sides would burst. Jokes he'd heard a hundred times before sounded fresh and new and even funnier. He had a feeling he couldn't explain to anyone. A feeling of belonging.

It was the best night he had ever had.

It was late when he got home. He hadn't told anyone he wouldn't be in and he fully expected a lecture from his parents. He was surprised when he didn't get one.

Glory pulled him into the living room. 'OK, where were you?' She had her hands on her hips and sounded exactly like his mother. 'They think you were with Tommy, stayed at his house for tea. But don't tell me you were there. I know different!'

'Who do you think you're talking to?' Kevin tried to walk out of the room, but Glory pulled him back.

'You let Tommy go to the dentist by himself. You knew he was relying on you. You're one rotten kind of friend.'

The dentist! He remembered and felt ashamed. He'd forgotten all about Tommy. But the shame was quickly pushed aside by his annoyance at being told off by Glory.

'You belt up!' he said. 'It's none of your business.'

'You went off with Salom, didn't you? So, where did you go?'

'You know so much, Sherlock, figure it out for yourself.' With that he left her, heading for the kitchen. He suddenly realized how hungry he was. His mother had made soup. Thick, luscious lentil soup, and there was crusty bread on the table. He was just about to tuck into a steaming bowl of it when his father came into the kitchen and completely ruined his appetite.

'Ah, there you are, son,' he said, rubbing his hands together. 'Not get fed well enough at Tommy's? But then, who can resist your mother's lentil soup?'

Kevin had just taken the first mouthful. His dad continued, 'So, are you coming with us on Saturday?'

Saturday! So much had happened to him, he had completely forgotten the horror that was to befall them on Saturday. Line dancing in the shopping mall.

'You're not serious. Tell me you're not serious.'

'Very serious, son. El Diablo and Honey Sue are dancing for the local children's hospital. A very worthy cause.'

'Could you not do something less embarrassing?' Kevin suggested. 'Like running naked through the town centre?'

His father laughed heartily. 'I knew you'd see the funny side eventually. You know what I always say, laughter is the best medicine.'

'Well, could you not do a bit of stand-up comedy instead then?'

His dad ignored that. 'Line dancing's great fun, Kevin. You should try it.'

'I'd rather stick needles up my nose,' he said seriously.

Glory came into the kitchen and sat across from him as their dad left. 'I'm going to die of embarrassment, Kevin,' she said. 'Maybe we could emigrate before Saturday.'

Their mother came into the kitchen just then. 'No, you'll be there. Both of you. Give your dad and me some moral support. After all,' she added wickedly, 'we went to all the embarrassing events at your school. Remember, Glory? The time your knickers fell down at the Christmas concert?'

Glory's face went bright red. 'Mum! You promised you'd never mention that again!'

Kevin roared with laughter. He'd been there too. It had been a great night.

His mum pointed an accusing finger at him. 'And don't you forget the time you wet yourself at the nativity play. And you playing Joseph too!'

'Mum!' he yelled. 'I was only six. You're allowed to wet yourself when you're only six.'

'Yes, dear,' she said with a smirk, 'but not all over baby Jesus's crib. So –' she continued as if she'd made her point – 'I'm sure we're not going to embarrass you half as much as that.'

Just then his dad appeared at the kitchen door. He was dressed in his full El Diablo outfit. He looked like an extra from a third-rate cowboy film.

'Come along, Honey Sue. A dress rehearsal for me and you?'

They both laughed and danced out of the kitchen. Kevin looked at Glory. Her face was still bright red. They were both thinking the same thing. Saturday was definitely going to be the most embarrassing day of their lives.

11

*T*ommy wasn't waiting for him at the corner next morning. Kevin didn't blame him. It was, as Glory had said – and how he hated agreeing with her – a rotten thing to have done.

Why had he done it? It wasn't like him to be so thoughtless.

So the first thing he did when he went into the playground was to search out Tommy and apologize.

Tommy just shrugged. 'Doesn't matter. Don't need you to go to the dentist with me. Don't need anybody.'

'So, how did you get on?'

Tommy didn't answer for a minute. He bent down and tied the laces of his trainers. 'Well, I didn't actually go.'

Kevin couldn't help it. He laughed. 'You wimp!'

Tommy took it in good part. He laughed too. 'I hate the dentist. I'm absolutely petrified.'

'I promise I'll go with you next week.'

Tommy stopped laughing abruptly and looked at him. A puzzled kind of look as if he was trying to figure something out. 'Will Salom let you?'

'I can do anything I want,' Kevin said, a bit annoyed.

'I don't like that Salom,' Tommy said.

'He's dead nice. Honest, Tommy. He's a really good laugh. You can trust him.'

Kevin knew he was gushing but couldn't help it. He couldn't understand why it was so important to stick up for Salom.

'I've seen the graffiti,' Tommy went on. 'It's everywhere. "Salom is evil."' He said it slowly, as if he was trying make Kevin understand. 'I think he's scary.'

That made Kevin laugh. 'Scary? Come on, Tommy. The only thing you're scared of is the dentist. Salom's not scary.'

Tommy didn't say a word, waiting for Kevin to go on.

'People are jealous of him. That's why they say all those nasty things about him.'

Tommy still didn't look convinced. 'Are you one of the Tribe now?'

Kevin had always said he'd never join a gang, so how could he explain to Tommy now how being in the Tribe made him feel? 'I suppose I am,' he said finally.

Tommy kicked at the ground. He looked disappointed. 'It's all going to change now for us.'

'No, it won't. Nothing will change.'

Tommy looked right at him. 'Tell me what the initiation test is then!'

A few days ago Kevin would have told Tommy anything. Hadn't that been his plan? Yet now he knew he couldn't tell him this. He had taken an oath. He couldn't let Torry down, or Salom, or even Doc. They had a common bond, the Walk of Death. How could he explain that to Tommy?

Tommy shrugged and walked off. 'And you think nothing's going to change.'

Salom was waiting for Kevin once again at the school gate. This time Tommy had gone home on his own. Maybe he was right. Things had changed.

Salom jumped off the wall to meet him. 'Came to tell you, we're all going to the island on Saturday.'

He didn't have to tell him what island. Cumbrae, the island in the middle of the river.

'Torry's granny's got a caravan there. We'll hire bikes. Have a brilliant time.'

'Sounds great to me . . .' Then he remembered the line dancing. He'd rather be cycling round the island with the Tribe, but he had promised. He had to go.

'What's wrong? Can't you go?'

Kevin wondered how Salom would react if he told him. Would he laugh, make a fool of him? No, he couldn't take the risk of being laughed at.

'Better be something really important,' Salom said. 'We do things together, the Tribe.'

'It's important for me.'

'Go on, tell me. No secrets, remember?'

Kevin stopped walking. He might as well tell him. Knowing El Diablo and Honey Sue, they would have the press there and their photograph would probably be plastered on the front page of the local paper.

So he told him everything.

Salom's reaction was exactly as Kevin had expected. He laughed so much he looked as if he was ready to cry. 'Line dancing! What a red face!'

'Thank you for that,' Kevin said. 'I needed you to laugh.'

Salom put his arm round his shoulders. 'Sorry, pal. But it is funny. Be honest.' He tried to stop chuckling. 'And you've got to be there to support them?'

Kevin nodded.

'Fair enough,' Salom said. 'We'll be there too then. To support you.'

That took Kevin by surprise. 'You will?'

'Sure. We're the Tribe, remember?'

He felt a little tingle of pride. The Tribe. 'What about the island?'

'We'll go another Saturday. The island's not going to move, is it?' He grinned. 'I'll see you on Saturday. At the mall.'

'Brilliant!' Kevin shouted after him. He felt better. Suddenly, Saturday wasn't going to be so bad after all.

12

'*A*re you sure they're not just coming to cause trouble?'

Why did Glory always have to put a spoke in every wheel? There he was, eating his dinner, watching his favourite television programme, and the only mistake he'd made was to tell Glory the Tribe were coming to the line dancing display.

'They wouldn't cause trouble. They're my friends.'

That didn't impress Glory. 'They've caused trouble before. When the Salvation Army played in the mall at Christmas they put chewing gum down their trombones and stuck their cymbals together.'

Kevin laughed. He'd thought that was funny at the time. Even before he had moved to this part of the town. Even before he was one of the Tribe.

But to do anything like that on Saturday, when it was so important to Mum and Dad. *No!* They wouldn't. He dismissed that thought. 'They won't cause any trouble. Trust me.'

'Will you introduce me to Salom?' Glory asked, looking excited at the prospect.

'No, I won't. You'll only embarrass me.'

'I'll make sure you introduce me.'

'I'll pretend I don't know you, squirt.'

'Nerd.'

He smirked. 'I'm not a nerd now. Now that I'm one of the Tribe.'

'They must be lowering their standards to let you in.'

It was building up to an argument. Added to that, Glory was putting him off his beefburgers. He lifted his plate and headed for the bedroom, and peace and quiet.

'You wait and see, Kevin Davidson. There will be trouble if they're there!'

And she was right.

There was trouble. But it didn't come from the Tribe.

At first Kevin thought they weren't going to come at all. The crowd in the mall was building up and Mum and Dad and the rest of their dance troupe were just about ready to start. But there was no sign of Doc or Torry or Salom.

He could see Glory with her friends at the other side of the mall. He had warned her not to come near him. He wasn't sure she would listen; she never had before. He tried to hide behind one of the telephone booths and hoped she wouldn't spot him.

The music began to ring out round the mall, tapes played on a machine by a DJ who was wearing a ten-gallon hat. The dancers lined up in three rows, all of them dressed in cowboy gear. El Diablo and Honey Sue were right at the front, leading the display. And no wonder, with all the practising they had put in. They could line dance for Britain.

The Tribe weren't coming after all. They were probably already cycling around the island, Kevin totally forgotten.

So much for friendship, for support, for . . .

The Tribe! Suddenly they were all racing towards him. He felt like whooping when he saw them. Torry had spotted him immediately and beckoned to the others to follow him. Salom loped along behind the rest and still managed to look as if he was leading

57

them. Doc, grim-faced – could he never manage a smile? – looked as if he'd rather be anywhere else than here.

'Not started yet?' Torry asked as he joined Kevin.

'Just about to,' Kevin answered.

Torry punched his arm. 'Dead embarrassing, eh?' Then he laughed. 'Never mind, we're here. It'll be a laugh.'

'Hi, Salom.' They gave each other a high hand salute. Doc hardly acknowledged him.

'Now, just promise me, no making a fool of them,' Kevin warned them all, adding, 'They're going to manage that fine by themselves.'

'Hey, maybe we'll enjoy it so much we'll want to join!' Torry did an intricate step and took a jump in the air. He landed with a thump on the ground. 'Maybe not. Think I'll stick to football.'

'Somebody's waving at you, Kev,' Salom said.

Kevin had been trying to ignore Honey Sue as she flapped her arms wildly to catch his attention. He looked behind him as if she must mean someone else.

'Wave to your mummy, Kev,' Salom said with a laugh, and he began to wave back at her. Torry did too, and soon all of the Tribe were waving and yelling at the line dancers.

Glory's words came back to him then. 'There will be trouble if they're there!' They wouldn't, surely. Yet he had a sinking feeling in the pit of his stomach that something was going to happen.

13

*I*t was at that moment that real trouble arrived. Glory.

'Hi, Kevin, are you trying to hide from me?' She was trying to look cute and failing miserably. It didn't help that her sweater was on inside out. Typical.

'This your baby sister, Kev?' Torry asked. He didn't wait for an answer. 'I'm Torry, Kev's pal. Pleased to meet you.'

Glory smiled back, but her eyes were on Salom. 'Are you the famous Salom?' she asked.

'Am I famous?'

'Well, I see your name written up everywhere,' Glory said, all innocence. 'But I've never seen anything nice written about you.'

Kevin cringed. 'Buzz off, Glory. You're an embarrassment.'

Salom only laughed. 'Glory? How did you get a name like that? Is it short for Gloria?'

'No, it is not,' Kevin answered. 'My dad took one look at her ugly mug when she was born and yelled "Glory Be!"'

Even Doc managed a smile at that one.

'No, he did not. My dad thought I was beautiful.'

'Yes, but our dad's got rotten eyesight. He does wear beer-bottle glasses.'

They all looked, and there he was, adjusting them on his face, so they wouldn't fall off when his dancing got too frenetic. Then his thumbs were stuck in the waistband of his trousers, which seemed the only way they could actually line dance, and his feet began tapping out the rhythm of the music on the tiles of the mall. Left right, left right. Gradually, the rest of the dancers fell into step with him, and with a wild cowboy holler the line dancing display began.

Kevin had never been so embarrassed in all his life. He watched his dad's face and he could see by his beaming smile that he was really enjoying himself. He wasn't embarrassed at all. How could that be? He used to be a perfectly sensible man, before line dancing had come into his life.

Torry began to clap in time with the music. 'Go on, yourself, Mr Davidson!'

He wasn't being sarcastic, Kevin could tell that. Salom began to clap too. Then the rest of the Tribe, even Doc, joined in. Suddenly, Saturday at the shopping mall didn't seem to be such a nightmare. Kevin began clapping too, and before they knew it all the shoppers in the mall had joined them.

When they finished their first dance the place erupted with applause.

'Hey, they're good,' Salom said, and added with a grin, 'for a bunch of oldies.'

'Yeah, we'll probably have to revive them in an

oxygen tent after this,' Kevin said, laughing.

Glory tried to join in the joke. 'Or maybe even put them in a . . .' She paused, thinking. 'What do you call them things you put people in to help them to breathe?'

His sister was unbelievable. 'An oxygen tent, stupid! I'm just after saying that.'

Glory was nonplussed. 'Is it not an iron lung?' she said.

Salom couldn't stop laughing. 'She's brilliant, Kev.'

'Brilliant?' Kevin said. 'She's as daft as a brush.'

The music began again. People took up the clapping straight away this time, already in the mood for more dancing.

It was then that Kevin spotted the Rebels. He recognized MacAfee first and nudged Salom. His nod told him he had already seen them.

'They look as if they want trouble,' he said. And they did. It was the way they were circling the dancers, watching them intently. They began to spread out around them. There was something threatening in the very way they moved.

'Watch them!' Salom ordered. No need to tell Kevin that. He couldn't take his eyes off them.

They all had their hands in their pockets and that struck Kevin as odd.

His eyes were drawn to MacAfee. They were all watching him, as if for some signal. And when it came, Kevin saw it too.

A wink, a nod, and in that second the hands came

out of the pockets and in each of them was a handful of marbles. They threw them simultaneously in the path of the dancers. Suddenly, the floor of the mall was a sea of tumbling marbles. There was a gasp from the crowd as one of the younger girls, not quite sure of her steps anyway, found herself dancing on a rolling, moving ball. She began to lose her balance; her arms began to flail wildly. She reached out to the girl beside her, grabbed her sleeve, and when she went down, she took the other girl with her.

Kev saw his dad glance behind him, not quite aware of what was happening, just as two more dancers lost their footing and toppled in a heap on the tiles. It was then that the rolling marbles reached his dad. He reached out for Honey Sue, but just too late, and when he crashed to the ground, so did she. The dancers were screaming, the crowd was yelling. The display had turned into a disaster. The line dancing was in chaos.

Kevin pushed through the crowd to his parents. He was so angry that, in that moment, he hated the Rebels. Hated what they'd done. He would have done anything to get his revenge on them. Especially on MacAfee.

His dad was still on the ground when he reached him, his glasses askew on his face. 'Are you all right, Dad?' he asked, helping him to his feet.

'I'm fine. Help your mum.'

But Salom was already there, helping Honey Sue to her shaky feet. She was almost in tears. 'The blinking little so-and-sos! They've ruined everything.'

'No, they haven't.' It was Salom who spoke. 'We'll get all the marbles brushed up. We'll all help.' He looked around, taking in not just the rest of the Tribe, but all the shoppers in the mall. 'Won't we?'

There was a general murmur of agreement.

'Once we do that, you can begin again.' He smiled at Honey Sue. 'You're all right, Mrs Davidson?'

She stood up straight. 'Indeed I am, son. And you're quite right. We're not going to let those little toerags spoil our day!'

And nor they did. Everyone in the mall helped, chasing marbles until it became as much fun as the line dancing itself. And the line dancing turned out to be a triumph. The crowd clapped and sang, and some even joined in. And at the end the charity boxes passed round by the dancers were filled to overflowing.

It was one of the best days ever. Thanks to Salom, and the Tribe.

'That was a great day!' Kevin said as they walked home.

'Better fun than cycling round the island,' Torry agreed. 'It was raining anyway.' Then he added, 'But we've got to get the Rebels back. We're not going to let them get away with that.' He let out a whoop of joy at the prospect. 'Revenge!' he yelled.

The word sent shivers down Kevin's spine.

Revenge.

14

'*Y*ou'll have to invite that nice boy home for tea some night, Kevin.'

Kevin looked at his mother, puzzled. 'What nice boy?'

'The one who saved the day at our line dancing display.' She giggled. 'Oh, listen to me. I'm a poet.'

Glory laughed too. 'His name's Salom, and we're inviting him home. Oh dear, I'm a poet too.'

Kevin had long ago decided all his family were candidates for the funny farm. But this was worse than usual. Poetry . . . at Sunday breakfast? It was too much.

'I'm not inviting him home,' he said. 'You lot embarrass me.'

Glory looked offended. 'Salom likes me.'

'He thinks you're an idiot.'

Nothing fazed Glory. 'He said I was brilliant.'

'A brilliant idiot,' Kevin said.

Glory turned to her mother. '*I'll* ask him.'

That was the last straw. 'No you will not! OK. OK. I give up. I'll ask him.'

Better if he asked him than Glory did or, even worse, Honey Sue in her western outfit.

His dad had been sitting reading the paper,

apparently oblivious to their conversation. Some chance! He peered over his glasses. 'Who are these boys you were with yesterday anyway, Kevin?'

'Just friends. Salom, Doc, Torry,' he replied.

Glory, of course, had to open her big mouth. 'They're the Tribe, Dad. They're the top gang around here. Kevin's one of them now.'

She let out an 'Ouch!' as Kevin kicked her under the table. Would she never learn how to keep quiet?

'A gang?' Dad put down his paper. He looked worried. 'You're in a gang, Kevin?'

Even the kick hadn't taught Glory a lesson. 'I don't know how he got in, Dad. The Tribe is dead cool, and look at our Kevin. He's a nerd.'

'Who are you calling a nerd, dog breath?'

'Right! That's enough!' His dad sounded angry. 'Kevin, you always said you wouldn't get caught up in any of these gangs. You were too sensible.'

'It's different from what you think, Dad. They're not really a gang . . . like the kind of gangs you mean.' It didn't sound convincing even to Kevin.

'Yes, they are. They were the first gang, and they're the best.' Glory glared at him as she said it, daring him to kick her again. He almost did.

'Kevin, I don't like the idea of this at all.'

Kevin stood up. He was out of here. 'I promise, Dad, it won't change me. You saw for yourself today. They're nice guys. We just have fun. They're my friends.'

'And what about Tommy?' his dad asked. 'I didn't see him there today.'

'No, he wasn't.' At first Kevin was going to make excuses for Tommy, feeling guilty that he hadn't even asked him to come. Then he changed his mind. 'He should have been there.' He was more sure of himself now. 'He knew I didn't want to go. He could have been there with me. But the Tribe came, and if it hadn't been for them the whole day would have been a disaster.'

He didn't want to hear any more. He knew his dad still wasn't happy about the situation, probably never would be. 'Look, I've got to go.'

His mother called after him. 'Don't forget to invite that boy.'

So he did, later that day as they sat outside the video shop munching chips.

'Tea at the Davidsons'?' Salom said, a big smile on his face. 'Sure thing. Sounds great.'

Kevin was surprised and pleased. He'd expected him to laugh outright. 'D'you mean it?'

'Sure. I think your family's brilliant, Kevin. Wait till you meet mine. The Family from Hell.'

He spat out a chip and suddenly, though he was still smiling, the smile wasn't in his eyes any longer.

The Family from Hell? What could he mean?

'I'll try and have Glory kidnapped for the night,' Kevin promised. 'She's bound to put you off your food.'

Salom shook his head. 'No, no, don't do that. She's so funny. And she doesn't even think she's being funny. She kills me.'

'You don't have to live with her.'

They were still laughing when Torry, Doc and some of the others joined them.

'So, what are we going to do about the Rebels?' Torry asked.

'We don't have to do anything, do we?' Kevin's anger had long ago subsided. He couldn't imagine now why he'd been so determined on vengeance in the first place. 'I mean, we should be thanking them. Because of them it turned into a brilliant day. And my parents think you lot are the Magnificent Seven.'

They were all looking at him as if he were mad.

Doc spoke first. 'We let them off with this they'll think they can get away with anything.'

'We've got to show them we're the tops,' Torry said.

Salom's voice was solemn. 'Kev, they tried to ruin your parents' display because you're one of us now: one of the Tribe. And if anyone hurts one of the Tribe, they hurt us all. Remember the oath? We stick together, no matter what.'

Kevin didn't want revenge. Something deep inside told him whatever they did would be dangerous and futile and stupid. But the Tribe had been there for him when he needed them. Now it was his turn: his chance to prove that he was worthy to be one of them.

'All right,' he said at last. 'What are we going to do to them?'

Salom grinned. 'I've come up with a brilliant plan.'

15

*K*evin pressed himself against the wall. He'd never been so scared in his life. Why was he here? he kept thinking. He didn't want revenge. That feeling had passed in an instant. Yet here he was, with the rest of the Tribe, waiting to ambush the Rebels.

Ambush! Was he crazy?

Only weeks ago he had thought the gangs acted as if they lived in an old Clint Eastwood western. He had laughed at them. Now he was one of them.

There was a sudden noise from the dark alley. What was it? Stones being kicked? He held his breath. He knew that somewhere in the gloomy doorways of this alley, Doc and Torry and the other members of the Tribe were, like him, pressed into the blackness, making themselves invisible.

Were they as scared as he was? Somehow he didn't think so.

When he'd heard the plan, Torry had been jubilant. 'Quality, man! Quality plan!' he had yelled. 'I can't wait.'

Doc, though unsmiling, seemed equally enthusiastic. He was the one who had suggested the alley as the perfect place to hide.

No, Kevin couldn't imagine they'd be afraid. Doc knew *he* was, however.

For once his mouth had curved into a smile as he taunted him. 'Will you be able to manage that night, or will you have to stay home with your mummy?'

He could never show Doc he was afraid. So he stayed there, holding his breath, his heart beating like a drum, and he waited.

And the plan? That was simple. So simple Kevin was sure it wouldn't work. Even the Rebels wouldn't be that stupid.

Salom was the decoy, leading them into the trap.

'Let me be the decoy!' Torry had pleaded.

But that wouldn't work so well, Salom had explained. 'It has to be me. MacAfee hates me. If he sees me alone, right in the middle of Rebel territory, he'll chase me for sure. They'll all chase me. And I'll lead them to you.'

'But what if they catch you?' Kevin had asked, and Salom had turned to him as if he'd just said something funny.

'Catch me? Catch Salom?'

Torry gave Kevin a push. 'You've never seen Salom run. Nobody runs like Salom.' Salom was Torry's hero.

Nobody runs like Salom. Well, Kevin hoped no one was going to expect *him* to run too fast. Running was not his strong point.

A sound. In the distance. Kevin strained his ears to hear it. Getting louder, closer. Yes. Feet running, splashing through puddles. Then more feet and cries and yells.

Closer.

The chase was on.

And suddenly, Salom raced into view. Kevin could just make out his features caught by a dim light hanging over one of the buildings. His smile was gone, replaced by a grim determination. And boy, Torry was right, Salom could run!

He moved like an athlete, all his concentration on speed. Faster and faster, with his jacket flying behind him.

All at once the Rebels were behind him, like a pack of hunting dogs chasing a rabbit. The Rebels, with MacAfee at the front.

'We'll get him!' he yelled, egging the rest of the gang on. Not that they needed much persuasion. Here was the notorious Salom, alone, and they were closing in on him.

Or they thought they were.

Salom whizzed past the doorway. On his heels, the Rebels. Kevin moved even further into the darkness. It wasn't time. Not yet.

Doc's high-pitched whistle was the signal for the Tribe to emerge from the doorways. When it came, seconds later, Kevin didn't even think. He was off, and he joined in the tribal roar as they raced after the Rebels.

The Rebels were no longer the hunters. They were the hunted.

The roar behind them took them totally by surprise. Some of them stumbled as they turned to see what was happening. MacAfee glanced back, and his face was something to see. He'd been tricked. He was furious, but he was also afraid.

'When they realize they're trapped,' Salom had said, 'they'll run. Scatter in all directions. So watch MacAfee. He's the one we're after. When we get him, we get our revenge.'

He was right. In a panic, the Rebels forgot Salom. They ran, trying to find a path through the Tribe. The other members of the Tribe chased after the Rebels. But Salom, Doc, Torry and Kevin ringed MacAfee. It was MacAfee Salom wanted. And suddenly MacAfee was alone and trapped. Salom had led him deliberately into a blind alley. It led nowhere. When MacAfee realized there was nowhere for him to run, he turned, ready to fight. Yet he was afraid. Kevin could see it in his eyes.

What were they going to do to MacAfee now? He hadn't asked. Hadn't followed the plan that far. Now they had MacAfee in their power and could do anything to him.

And what really frightened Kevin was the fact that he liked the feeling. Here was the boy who had tried to ruin his parents' day. Here was the boy who had been ready to do anything to him in the underground car park. He'd been so arrogant then.

Well, he wasn't arrogant now.

As Salom stepped in front of him, MacAfee licked the sweat from his lips.

'Thought you had me, eh?' Salom taunted him. 'Not this time. Not ever.' Salom didn't take his eyes off him. He called back to the others, 'So, what are we going to do with him?'

Doc looked at Kevin. 'You decide,' he said. 'We're doing this for you.'

Salom agreed. 'Yes, Kev, you decide.'

He could tell them to do anything to MacAfee, and he knew they would do it.

MacAfee was totally in his power, and MacAfee was afraid.

16

'OK, we're waiting. What are we going to do with him?'

Doc sounded impatient. Only seconds had passed since he'd first asked, but those seconds had taken ages to drag by.

Power. That was what Kevin had. Power over MacAfee.

Kevin looked at MacAfee. MacAfee couldn't take his eyes off Kevin. He swallowed nervously, and beads of sweat formed on his brow.

Kevin had never liked this boy. He had a cruel streak in him. If he had caught Kevin in the same situation . . . in his power . . . Kevin shook the thought away. MacAfee would have no mercy. But Kevin wasn't MacAfee. He could never be like him. He never wanted to be.

At that moment his eye was caught by a swinging door to the left of MacAfee. It flapped open, belonging to one of the derelict shops in the alley. TO LET was painted in cracked lettering on the front. Then Kevin realized that what it actually said was TOILET, but the 'I' was missing.

'Take him over there,' he said, nodding toward the door.

Salom and Doc grabbed MacAfee. He struggled, but he wasn't strong enough to fight against both of them. Torry danced with glee towards the door. Suddenly he stopped. 'It is stinking in there!' He held his nose.

So it was. The stench hit them all at the same time. Some old tramps must still be using this, but now the toilets didn't flush. Disgusting.

'I'm not going in there!' Torry said, taking a step back.

'No, you're not,' Kevin agreed. 'But he is.' He turned to MacAfee. 'Don't worry. It'll only be for an hour or two.'

MacAfee's eyes widened in horror. Physical pain would be better than this. 'You're not serious!' he yelled. 'You're not putting me in there.'

Salom was laughing now too. 'Yes, in with the other turds, MacAfee.' He began pushing the boy into the toilet.

MacAfee exploded with rage. He lashed out and

caught Doc in the eye with his fist. Doc fell back and let go of him, but Salom still held him fast.

'Help me, Kev!' he shouted. Kevin grabbed MacAfee's arm and pushed him with all his strength. MacAfee tripped and fell headlong between two of the open cubicles. He gagged from the smell, tried to stand up but was not quick enough. Kevin, Doc and Torry slammed the door shut on him and leaned their combined weight against it.

'How do we keep him in there?' Torry shouted.

Kevin glanced around. There was an old cooker dumped in a corner. 'Can we push that against the door?' he said breathlessly.

Doc and Torry struggled to lift it and drag it closer. All the while MacAfee was thumping the door and shouting all sorts of horrible abuse at them.

Finally, they managed to wedge the door tight with the old cooker. 'Gotya, MacAfee!' Salom shouted.

MacAfee was going crazy inside. He banged ferociously on the door. 'Let me out! It's stinking in here.'

'Well, you should feel at home then. You're stinking as well,' Kevin called back.

'I'll get you all for this!' MacAfee threatened.

'We're shaking in our shoes, aren't we, boys?' Salom laughed.

MacAfee was breathless with anger. 'You all think Salom's so smart! Ask him what happened to Stash.'

For a second the smile slipped from Salom's face. But only for a second.

'Shut up, MacAfee! Nobody's listening to you!'

74

'Don't worry, we'll make sure you get out soon,' Kevin shouted. 'And by that time you'll be used to the smell.'

'I'll pay you back for this, Davidson. You'll be sorry.'

But by now no one was listening. They howled with joy. Their revenge was complete.

They ran down the alley with MacAfee's pounding still ringing in their ears.

'That was brilliant!' Salom yelled.

'We can always outsmart the Rebels.' Torry laughed. 'That's why we're the best.'

Kevin couldn't deny it was a good feeling. And they hadn't done anything really bad. MacAfee would be free and safe, if a little smelly, very soon.

At the shopping precinct they came across two of the Rebels. They didn't look too anxious for a fight now. When they saw the Tribe coming towards them they stepped back, ready to run.

Salom held up his hands. 'No worries,' he said, as if he was their best friend. 'Just came to let you know your great leader needs rescuing. I think he got himself locked in the loo, up that alley where you chased me.'

Now Kevin and Torry, and even Doc, were laughing too.

'And take some toilet paper!' Torry called after them as they ran off. 'I think he might need it.'

As soon as he knew that MacAfee would be freed, Kevin felt better. He couldn't help it. Now he could really enjoy his revenge.

Salom didn't miss the change in him. 'You know, Kev, if he'd caught me in that alley, he would have done a lot worse than locking me in a stinking toilet for half an hour.'

Kevin knew that too. 'But we're not like him. You're not like him.'

Torry leapt in the air and punched nothing. 'Salom's the best. There's nobody to beat Salom.'

Salom swung him round and round. 'My fan club. Torry!'

Doc was silent. He strode on ahead as if he wasn't with them now. If Salom noticed, he didn't remark on it. But Kevin noticed and wondered.

Soon, Doc and Torry were heading off for home, but Salom stayed with Kevin and they walked on together in quiet, comfortable friendship.

'Good night, eh?' Salom asked.

'It was a great night.' And he meant it. Now it was over, like the Walk of Death, even the fear seemed exciting. The chase, tricking the Rebels. Watching their faces when they realized the Tribe was after them, trapping MacAfee. It was all exciting now.

'We'll have a thousand nights like that, Kev,' Salom promised. 'Now you're one of the Tribe.' Then his face became serious. 'But don't forget what MacAfee said. We'll have to watch him. He won't rest till he gets his revenge on you.'

That Kevin believed, but at the moment he wasn't worried about MacAfee.

'What did he mean, about Stash?' Kevin asked

him. It had been bothering him since MacAfee had said it.

Salom shook his head. 'Maybe he was trying the Walk of Death again. Who knows?'

'But why would he try it a second time?'

Salom lifted his shoulders and shrugged. He moved off, heading for home. 'How would I know?' he said. 'I wasn't there.'

Then he was gone. A shadow, hurrying off down the dark streets.

Salom.

17

'*H*ey, do you eat like this all the time?' Salom stood in the dining room, surveying the table set for five, with sparkling cutlery and glasses and a crisp, white embroidered tablecloth.

'Yes, 'fraid so,' Kevin apologized.

'What do you mean, "'Fraid so"? I think it's brilliant. I only ever have something on my knee in front of the telly.'

'On a plate, I hope,' said Glory, emerging from the kitchen with a jug of iced water.

'Oh, hello, Glory. Can I help?'

'It would be a lot safer than Glory helping,' Kevin said. 'She usually breaks something.'

'I do not!' Glory insisted, and immediately bumped into Dad coming out of the kitchen with the gravy. Brown spots splashed all over him.

'It's OK,' he said, 'it's only my good shirt.'

Glory flounced on to a chair and folded her arms. She wasn't going to help any more.

Suddenly, Kevin noticed the ponytail. She glanced up and saw him studying her in alarm.

With a wicked smile, she pointed to the white band wrapped round her hair.

'Ruffle! Ruffle! Ruffle!' she chanted.

Salom looked puzzled.

'Private joke, Salom,' Kevin told him.

They all took their seats at the table. Kevin wondered if Salom really thought all this was simply for his benefit. He would have to assure him later that it wasn't.

'So, how's the line dancing going, Mrs Davidson?' Salom asked.

Kevin nudged him. 'Don't ask. They're liable to give us a demonstration after tea.'

Salom laughed. 'I wouldn't mind. I think you're family's brilliant, Kev.'

'Do you?' Kevin was surprised, and pleased. His dad with his beer-bottle glasses, his mum and her line dancing. He never thought that someone as cool as Salom would consider them 'brilliant'. 'They're all right, I suppose,' he admitted.

'Pity about your sister,' Salom said.

'Yeah, but you can't have everything.'

Glory sat up straight. 'And what do you mean by that?'

'I read a book once –'

Before Salom could continue, Glory butted in. 'Oh, congratulations. I've read two.'

Salom ignored her and went on. 'It was about this man who had a mad wife in his attic. Now you, Kevin, haven't got a mad wife –'

'But I have got a mad sister!' Kevin finished for him. The two boys thought this was highly amusing. Glory's face was grim. She was trying to make an impression on Salom, and her brother was doing nothing to help her.

Kevin just couldn't let it go. 'We haven't got an attic to keep her in, unfortunately,' Kevin said through a guffaw. 'We let her roam about free. She's harmless really.'

Glory turned to her mother. 'They're being really nasty to me, Mum,' she complained.

Mrs Davidson, however, thought it was all just as amusing. 'They're only kidding, dear. You're too sensitive. Now, eat before it gets cold.'

Chicken was on the menu tonight, but Glory had her eternal favourite, macaroni cheese. Salom watched as she munched into it as if she hadn't eaten for days. 'Are you a vegetarian, Glory?'

'She's just always loved her macaroni and cheese, Salom,' Mum said fondly.

'In fact, she eats so much –' Kevin laughed – 'I don't think it's brains she's got, it's a head full of cheesy pasta!'

Now Salom was laughing too. 'That explains every-thing then!'

Glory sat in a huff. She sucked in her cheeks and wouldn't look at anyone.

'I think you're brilliant, Glory,' Salom said.

Glory immediately beamed a smile at him. She could never not smile for long. 'Do you?'

Kevin tutted. 'I see you don't need much convinc-ing.'

Glory ignored him. She kept smiling at Salom. Kevin thought she was beginning to look stupid. And at that instant he realized that his sister had a crush on Salom. Yuck! It made him feel sick.

'So, if I'm brilliant, can I join the Tribe as well?'

Why did Glory always have to open her mouth and put both feet and a couple of shoes in it? Mr Davidson stopped eating his chicken and looked at her. Then his gaze went to Salom and Kevin.

'I'm going to tell you right now,' he said, waving his knife at them, 'I don't like the idea of gangs. I don't like Kevin being in one and he knows that. I think you're too sensible to be in one as well, Salom. You're unique. Kevin's unique. You join a gang and you're just one of the crowd. Be your own person.'

Kevin closed his eyes. Here it came, one of his dad's little sayings.

'To thine own self be true,' he quoted.

Oh dear, he had forgotten to tell Salom about his dad's little sayings.

Dad turned his attention to Glory. 'And as for you,

young lady –' To make his point he waved his fork with a sliver of roast chicken on it in front of her – 'I don't want to hear another word about you joining a gang!'

Anyone with any sense would have just let it go. Salom did. So did Kevin. But then, Glory didn't have any sense.

After dessert, when Mum and Dad were in the kitchen making coffee, she was at it again. 'Can I join?'

'Girls aren't allowed in the Tribe,' Salom explained.

'Anyway, you'd never pass the initiation test,' said Kevin, and Salom kicked him under the table.

That made Glory even more defiant. 'Anything a boy can do, I can do.'

'You're not getting in!' Both boys said it at the same time and then laughed uproariously.

All in all, Salom made a big impression on Kevin's family, especially his mother and his sister. His dad, Kevin could tell, was wary. The Tribe bothered him. But Kevin and Salom would prove that being in a gang was nothing to worry about.

When Salom left, the boys stood at the door for a long time just talking and laughing.

'I had a great time tonight, Kev,' Salom told him.

'I thought you'd be bored. I thought you'd just eat and run,' Kevin said.

Salom shook his head. 'You don't know what it feels like to be with a normal family, a nice family.' For a moment he didn't say a word, as if he couldn't find the right words to say. 'You don't know how lucky you are, Kevin,' he said after a long pause, and there was so much sadness in his voice. 'You'll understand when you meet my family.'

Kevin watched him stride down the street, sure of himself, a little arrogant maybe, yet somehow vulnerable. 'You'll understand when you meet my family.' And Kevin remembered what Salom had called them: 'The Family From Hell'.

18

Nothing was ever as much fun as those next few weeks with the Tribe: chases with the other gangs, mischief in the mall, getting up to all sorts of tricks and games. Nothing bad, Kevin convinced himself. What was so wrong with playing football on the bowling green? Or riding their bikes at night over the local golf course? Fun, that was all it was.

There were new games to be learned, exciting games, dangerous games. But, after the Walk of Death, nothing seemed dangerous any more. Anyway, they were the Tribe, with a reputation to uphold. A reputation that they were afraid of nothing.

Kevin, who had always been the sensible one, the down-to-earth schoolboy, was caught up in the sheer exhilaration of being one of them.

'I never thought I'd see the day when you'd be a member of a gang, Kevin,' Mr Lever at the paper shop said. 'You disappoint me.'

Kevin didn't like disappointing people, but they just didn't understand. 'It's not like you think,' he tried to explain. 'We just have fun together. Great fun.'

But no one understood. No one.

You had to be one of the Tribe to understand. The feeling that you were the best – how could Kevin ever explain that?

He left his job at the newsagent's anyway. There wasn't time to deliver papers, not when all the rest of the Tribe were off on one of their exploits.

He didn't have time for homework either. And that he couldn't explain.

'You're grounded if you don't start working harder at school, Kevin,' his mother said. She tried to keep things from his dad. But she wouldn't do that for ever.

Dad noticed anyway. 'I told you these gangs were nothing but trouble,' he said. He was becoming increasingly worried and anxious about the changes he saw in Kevin. But what changes? Kevin thought. The only changes in him were for the better. He felt alive. Really alive.

But he promised to keep up with his homework if they would just leave him alone about the Tribe. He'd stay out of trouble, he assured them.

That was more difficult than he thought.

'Let's skip school tomorrow,' Salom said one night as they sat in the mall. 'The weather's great and we could go up the hill to the old reservoir. Have a cook-out. Swim.'

Torry jumped in the air. 'Brilliant! It's been ages since we did that. We could build a fire. Boil spuds. I'll bring the pot.'

'And I'll bring the spuds,' Doc said, almost enthusiastically. He looked at Kevin. 'What do you say?'

Inside, Kevin was groaning. He had only just promised his mum and dad to behave, not let the Tribe interfere with his schoolwork, and here he was, being asked to take a whole day off school. He'd never done that before. Never been the type to do it.

'It's only one day,' Salom said, as if he could read Kevin's mind. 'No one will ever know.'

'Will you get into trouble from Mummy?' Doc said in that sarcastic way of his. 'So will I. I always do. But I'm willing to risk it.'

Torry laughed. 'You boys and your problems with parents! You should have a mum and dad like mine. They don't give a big green bogey what I do.'

With that he drew one out from somewhere deep inside his brain and flicked it over their heads.

'Gross, Torry!' Doc yelled, laughing.

He shrugged almost with pride.

Salom said nothing. Would his parents mind if they found out?

'I'll have to bribe Glory to keep her mouth shut,' Kevin said, and knew then that he'd already decided.

'Tell her she can be our mascot,' Salom said with a grin.

'More like our unlucky charm,' Kevin said.

So it was decided, and Kevin went home excited, and something else – that 'something else' feeling he had only with the Tribe.

The next day dawned cloudless and hot. Even in the early morning workmen in the street were labouring, stripped to the waist. Women sat in their gardens having breakfast, dressed in shorts, enjoying the late summer heatwave.

Kevin, armed with bottles of lemonade and crisps, met Salom and the others at the chippy and together they began the long trek up the hill, over the burn, through bracken and swamps, heading for the reservoir. It was a long, arduous walk, but that didn't matter. The walk itself was part of the fun. Torry was at his best, telling jokes so stupid they couldn't stop laughing at them. Even Doc was smiling.

The reservoir was deserted and quiet, except for a wood pigeon somewhere in the distance hooting an early morning call. They threw themselves on the grass and surveyed the view. It was breathtaking. The reservoir overlooked the town and the river, and from here they could see all the way down to where the estuary opened out to the Irish Sea. And across the river, the hills and bens, purple and majestic, rolling one behind the other to the horizon.

'This is a brilliant place to live,' Kevin said, and meant every word.

'It's a dump,' Torry claimed. 'My dad told me.'

'That's because your dad hasn't worked since you

were born, and the only view he ever appreciated was the bottom of a bottle.'

Kevin waited for Torry to jump on Doc in defence of his dad. Instead, he only laughed. 'Never said a truer word, Doc.'

'You see things different, Kev,' Salom said. 'You see good things when everybody else only sees the bad.'

His dad had instilled that in him. 'Look for beauty in everything, Kevin, and beauty is what you'll find.'

'Some people call that being stupid.' This was Doc. His smile had gone. Some day, Kevin decided, he would ask Doc why he disliked him so much. Some day, but not today.

Today was meant only for fun.

'Let's swim!' Torry screamed, stripping right down to his trunks.

Danger signs were dotted all around the reservoir, warnings that swimming was forbidden. There had been drownings here, people caught up in the reeds and currents that lurked below the still waters.

Yet they ignored them. So did Kevin, sensible Kevin. He helped push the signs down and ran into the water as enthusiastically as the rest.

They splashed and swam and played and laughed as the sun rose higher and hotter and the morning wore on.

Kevin built the fire for them. 'Thank goodness for the Boy Scouts,' he laughed. And they filled the pot with water from the reservoir and threw in the potatoes. Then they lay in the long grass and told jokes and stories as they waited for the water to boil.

'Is this not the best time you've ever had?' Torry asked him.

He didn't even have to think about the answer. 'It sure is.'

The sun beat down, drying their trunks on them. Kevin drew in a deep breath, smelling the peat from the hills, and the pine trees, and the wood fire.

Memories, he thought, memories of a perfect day.

'This is a feast fit for a fat old king!' Salom joked as they ate their potatoes and beans, washed down with the lemonade.

'I don't want to eat anything but spuds and beans ever again!' Torry yelled.

Kevin agreed. Nothing had ever tasted so good.

'So, how did you bribe Glory?' Salom asked him later as they munched on crisps.

'Well, it wasn't easy.' He wasn't sure how they were going to take this. 'But I said she could come out with us one night.'

There was an immediate wail of protest from Doc. 'A girl?'

Kevin added quickly, 'Only for a couple of hours. It was the only way I could get her to take a note in to my teacher.' He watched for Salom's reaction. To his relief, Salom's face broke into a wide grin.

'No problem,' he said.

Torry agreed, but then he always did agree with Salom. 'If Salom says it's OK, it's OK with me.'

Doc still wasn't convinced. 'But his sister,' he moaned, 'she's as daft as a brush.'

Now that was exactly Kevin's opinion of Glory, but hearing it come from someone else annoyed him more than he expected. Maybe he did like his sister after all.

'She makes me laugh,' Salom said.

'I think she likes you too,' Kevin told him and was immediately sorry.

Torry sat bolt upright. 'Glory and Salom. Just like Romeo and Juliet.'

Salom lifted a half-eaten potato and threw it at him. Torry threw it back and Salom began to chase him through the long grass. Kevin joined them and so did Doc. They whooped like Apaches on the warpath, catching each other, fighting, laughing, until once again they were all in the water, splashing about and swimming.

In the late afternoon they gathered up their belongings and began to make their way round the old reservoir to the path that led back down to the town. A group of boys with pots and pans clanking in their rucksacks, their hair still damp from their swim; boys with not a care in the world.

Kevin stopped at the brow of the hill, looking back at the reservoir with the sun glittering like a thousand diamonds on the water, at the long grass swaying in the September breeze. He breathed in the clear air, filling his lungs. He listened to the birds, heard again the wood pigeon in some distant tree.

'What are you thinking?' Salom asked him.

'I'm remembering everything,' he said, not caring if it sounded stupid. Somehow he didn't think it would to Salom. 'Taking a picture in my mind. I don't ever want to forget today, Salom. This has been the best day of my life.'

19

'*H*ave you got to go home now?' Salom asked.

Doc and Torry had already gone their own way, with much laughter and shouting. Kevin and Salom were meandering the few short blocks till they would go their separate ways too.

Kevin didn't want the day to end. Never wanted it to end.

'No,' he said. 'I told Mum I'd be going to football practice after school.'

Truth was, football practice was a thing of the past. Football with the Tribe was so much more fun.

Lies and more lies, he thought. When had he become such an accomplished liar?

The Tribe had taken over his life.

Salom put his arm round Kevin's shoulder. 'Good. You can come back to my place.'

'You mean ... I'm actually going to meet the Family from Hell?'

Salom laughed. 'You'll be safe enough. A crucifix, some garlic, a wooden stake . . .'

Kevin stopped in his tracks. 'Hey, wait a minute. A family of vampires? Maybe I should just go home. Even Glory sounds better than that.'

They laughed and ran all the way to the block of walk-up apartments where Salom lived. His flat was on the third floor, at the end of a long balcony.

There were pots of flowers outside Salom's front door and, as soon as Kevin walked into the hall, the smell that hit him was of fresh flowers. Freesias and geraniums and roses. Bowls of flowers were on every window sill. Vases tumbling with colourful blooms. Whatever Kevin had imagined Salom's house to be like, nothing had prepared him for this. The flat was sparkling and clean and modern and fragrant.

'Someone sure likes flowers,' Kevin said.

'My mother.' Salom sounded as if he was apologizing. 'She always wanted a garden.'

'I think it's nice,' Kevin said truthfully.

As if on cue, a woman appeared from one of the rooms leading off the hall. Salom's mother. Kevin knew that right away. He looked like her. Same dark eyes, same shiny brown hair. She was younger than Kevin had expected, and really pretty.

She beamed a wide smile at them both. 'Oh, Salom. You've brought a friend. And what's your name?'

Before Kevin could answer she had turned her attention to her son. 'Did you have a nice picnic?'

His mother knew Salom hadn't gone to school, and she wasn't angry. That amazed Kevin.

'It wasn't a picnic!' Salom snapped. The smile that was always on his face had gone. 'What do you think we are, the Famous Five?'

He grabbed Kevin and pushed past his mother. 'We're going to play with the computer in my room.'

His mother fluttered behind them nervously. If Kevin had spoken like that to his mother, she'd be chasing him up the hall with a frying pan.

'Of course, dear. Do you want something to eat? Crisps? Nuts? Will I make you both some burgers?'

Salom turned on her at his bedroom door. 'No!' He almost shouted it. Then he closed the door firmly in her face. Kevin was shocked.

'Salom, that's your mother! I can't believe you spoke to her like that. She was being dead nice to you.'

Salom shrugged his shoulders. 'She's always dead nice to me. I could kick her downstairs and she'd apologize for getting in my way.'

'Well, some mothers are like that,' Kevin said weakly.

'Yours isn't.' Salom switched on the computer.

'No,' Kevin admitted. 'By now, mine would have me hanging up by the ears.'

Salom sat on the swivel chair by the computer and swung round. 'You know, Kev, I used to do things just to see if she'd tell me off. She never did.'

'Some boys would sell their soul for a mother like that.'

'They can have mine,' Salom said, sounding as if he meant it.

'You talk as if you don't like her.'

Salom didn't answer at once. He was inserting a disk into the computer and, for a minute, Kevin didn't think he was going to answer at all.

'She's my mother,' he said finally.

However, as the night wore on, Kevin began to understand how she could get on your nerves. She was at the door every ten minutes, tapping, asking if they needed anything. Never actually coming in. Never daring to come in. It was almost as if she was afraid to annoy her son.

Yet annoying him was exactly what she was doing.

'Why can't she just leave me alone!' Salom said through gritted teeth. 'That's why I never bring friends here.'

'So, why did you bring me?'

'You're a special friend, Kevin. A best friend. I've never had a best friend before.'

'What about Torry? Doc?'

'I don't think Doc even likes me. And as for Torry . . .' Salom hesitated.

Kevin answered for him. 'I know, a best friend is someone who can tell you if you're doing something wrong, as well as praise you for doing something right. Torry just thinks everything you do is right.'

'But you and me, Kev, we can talk to each other. Tell each other the truth. You are my best friend, aren't you?'

Kevin didn't hesitate. 'And you're mine,' he said.

Salom laughed then. 'So, this is your initiation test. You got to meet the Family from Hell.'

'This is worse than the Walk of Death!' Kevin laughed too. 'Hey, but I've only met your mother. What's your dad like?'

He found that out later. Suddenly, the door to the bedroom was flung open and a big, gruff man stood there. His face was grim. He didn't look at Kevin, only stared at the back of Salom's head, because Salom didn't turn to look at him.

'What are you doing inside? Why aren't you out? It's a beautiful day.'

He smelled as if he'd spent most of his beautiful day in the pub.

Salom didn't even answer him. He just continued to play the game.

Kevin began to stutter. 'We've been . . . eh, we're just going . . . eh . . .'

The man ignored him. He just stared at Salom's back in disgust.

'I suppose you've missed school again!' This time he didn't expect an answer. He just turned from them and left the room, slamming the door behind him. Only then did Salom swivel round to face Kevin. He was grinning. 'My beloved father. Isn't he delightful?'

'But, Salom, you weren't very nice to him either. People treat you the way you treat them.'

Goodness, he sounded just like his dad!

'He's always treated me like that. He hates me. He's always hated me.' Salom stood up. 'I'm stuck in the middle, Kevin. And I don't know why.'

For the first time, Kevin felt sorry for Salom. His own mum and dad were dead embarrassing at times, but they all had fun together and he knew they loved him. Kevin could never imagine any fun in this house.

That was when the shouting began somewhere in the flat. Salom's mother screeching at his father. His loud, angry voice, shouting back.

'Time to go,' Salom said with a sigh.

Salom stood at the door, waving, as Kevin hurried along the balcony to the stairs. The arguing could still be heard reverberating in the stillness of the night.

Kevin almost tripped over a woman coming out of her house with some rubbish. She glanced at Kevin, then let her eyes follow his wave to Salom, still standing in the doorway.

'You one of *his* pals?' she asked cheekily.

He almost told her he was his best friend, but it would have sounded stupid. So he simply nodded.

'Not for long, I bet.' Then her voice became a hoarse whisper. 'Just don't get on the wrong side of him, son. Bad things happen to people that get on the wrong side of that boy.' She stepped back into her doorway as if she was afraid that Salom might hear her. 'See, that boy,' she said mysteriously, 'he's got the evil eye.'

Kevin looked back at Salom's door, but he had gone.

The evil eye, indeed. What nonsense! Salom was his pal. His best pal. They'd had a great day together.

He was almost laughing as he turned on to the lower landing and saw it. There on the wall in front of him, in metre-high letters, the legend:

SALOM IS EVIL.

20

As soon as he walked in the door he knew something wasn't right. The silence, as if everyone had been waiting for him to come in.

'Hello, is anybody home?' he shouted.

His dad appeared from the living room. 'Oh, we're here all right,' he said ominously. 'You come in here, boy.'

Oh dear, that was not the friendliest of tones. Glory, he thought at once. She's messed it up again.

His mum and dad were sitting side by side on the sofa, not a smile on their faces. 'And where have you been?'

What was the point of telling them he'd been at football practice? They evidently knew he hadn't. He shrugged his shoulders.

His dad got to his feet and began pacing the room. 'Kevin! What's happening to you? Giving Glory a letter, a forged letter . . .'

So Glory had messed it up right enough.

'You forged my name!'

Kevin almost smiled. He thought he'd done that rather well. His dad was not amused. 'This is no laughing matter. You didn't go to school today. You lied.'

Again Kevin shrugged. 'I took a day off school. Boys do it all the time. It's not a big deal.'

Now his mum jumped to her feet. 'Not a big deal? You lied to us. A teacher phones to ask how you are, and I don't have a clue what she's talking about! We've always been able to trust you, Kevin.'

'You've changed since you joined that Tribe. I knew you would. How often have I told you, don't be a sheep, be a –'

'Oh, don't give me any more of your daft sayings, Dad.'

His dad's face fell. He was really hurt. For an instant Kevin felt guilty. But only for an instant. 'I took a day off school. You two are going on as if I robbed the Bank of England. I'm fed up with this!'

He made a move to leave the room. His dad pulled him back. 'You'll leave this room when I tell you, not before!'

'You are grounded, Kevin!'

Even as his mother said it, Kevin thought, I'd like to see you try!

He could lay bets that neither Doc nor Torry was getting this amount of hassle for a day off school.

'Ground me then!' he shouted at them. 'See if I care!'

But he wouldn't let them, he thought. If he had to climb out of a window, he'd be out with the Tribe. He stormed out of the room and this time his dad did nothing to stop him.

Glory was waiting in his bedroom for him. She was almost in tears. 'I've been grounded too, I hope you know.'

'Good!' he snapped at her. 'You deserve it. I might have known not to trust you.'

'It was your fault. You told me to give the teacher the note and say nothing. Well, I didn't say anything. Not really.'

He threw himself down on the bed. 'What do you mean, not really?'

'She asked what was wrong with you and I said I didn't know. That didn't sound very believable so I just added a bit.'

Here it comes, he thought, Glory's 'bit' that had ruined a perfect day.

Glory went on. 'I just said Mum and Dad wouldn't tell me what was wrong with you. They wouldn't even let me in to see you. I said that I thought maybe it was infectious.' She was warming to her story. 'And she asked if they'd got the doctor in, so I had to say "Yes". He'd come in the middle of the night and he was coming in again to see if your temperature had gone down.'

He could have screamed at her. A note explaining a summer cold had become a typhoid epidemic in her hands.

'She was so worried about you, she phoned home.'

What was the point of blaming her? Glory was Glory. He'd been a fool to trust her with such a mission. It was his own fault, really.

And Glory, being Glory, suddenly changed her mood and beamed a big, enthusiastic smile at him. 'Did you have a good day?' she asked.

And to his surprise, after everything that had happened, he told her all about it. It had been so special, so good, he wanted to share it with somebody. All except what happened at Salom's house. Somehow, he thought Salom wouldn't want him to share that with anybody.

Glory listened with rapt attention. 'Oh, Kev, I so want to be one of the Tribe.'

'Not that again! No way, Glory. You can spend one night with us, although you don't even deserve that after what's happened, and that's all.'

But somehow Glory's fate seemed to be tied up with the Tribe.

It was a few days later and Kevin and Doc, Torry and Salom were lounging about in the mall. He had ignored being grounded and that had caused even more problems at home. It was less hassle staying out with the Tribe.

Suddenly Tommy came running towards them. Tommy! Kevin hadn't seen him in a long time. Now at school they passed each other in the corridors with only a 'Hello'. His face was red and he was breathing hard as he raced in their direction. He looked as if he was almost ready to panic.

Kevin jumped to his feet. 'Tommy! What's the matter?'

Tommy stopped right in front of him, ignoring the rest of them. He could hardly get the words out.

'It's . . . Glory . . .' he said breathlessly. 'We came out of band practice together and then I thought she went off home. But I've just seen her. She's being chased by MacAfee and the Rebels.'

Glory was still grounded, but on band practice nights she was on a curfew.

Salom was on his feet in an instant. 'Where?' he shouted.

'Looked as if she was heading for the old pier.'

Glory run there? There was no escape from the pier, only the dark, cold river. Trust Glory!

'Come on,' Salom yelled.

And they all broke into a run behind him. Tommy too.

It was then that Salom stopped and turned. 'No. Not you. The Tribe will take care of this. It's our fight.' His eyes moved to Kevin, waiting for him to back him up.

Tommy looked at Kevin too. He was puzzled and hurt. 'I want to help, Kev.'

It was the cruellest thing Kevin had ever done. He couldn't even understand why he did it. 'Thanks for letting us know, Tommy,' he said, 'but we'll handle it now.'

He glanced at Salom, and there was a strange, satisfied smile on his face.

'What's happened to you, Kev?' Tommy called after him. 'You've changed. You've really changed.'

Later, he would think of those words, but not now. Now all he could think about was Glory.

Was this MacAfee's revenge on Kevin? If anything happened to that daft sister of his because of what he'd done, he'd never forgive himself.

His fear made him run faster, till he passed even Salom and was leading them through the mall and down towards the river.

Please, he prayed, don't let anything have happened to her. Please, let us be on time!

21

As they turned on to the old, dilapidated pier, he could see them silhouetted against the darkening skyline: a circle of Rebels, dancing, laughing, chanting.

But where was Glory? And in that instant Kevin saw her. She was tied to one of the old lamp posts, squirming to free herself and shouting all sorts of vengeance at MacAfee. Good old Glory, defiant as ever, he thought, surprised that he was almost proud of her.

Salom whizzed past him with a roar and in a second was in the middle of them. He shouldered one out of the way, then another. Taken by surprise, they stumbled and fell. Salom headed straight for Glory, untying her.

'We were only having a bit of fun,' MacAfee said. His whole stance was wary, ready for anything, a fight, or a chase.

'Not with Glory,' Salom said.

Kevin saw his sister's face transformed from defiance and anger to adoration when Salom said that. It was most embarrassing.

'Take Glory home,' Salom shouted at Kevin.

'I want to stay,' Glory insisted, shaking herself free of Salom's grip.

But Salom was having none of that. 'You're going home,' he said.

'What are you going to do?' Kevin asked.

Salom grinned. 'Have a bit of fun, just like they were going to do with Glory.'

Kevin didn't want to go, but he certainly didn't want his sister there. He had no choice. He took Glory by the arm and began pulling her up the pier.

He glanced back. Most of the Rebels had run off; only MacAfee was left with two of his gang. They were held by Torry and Doc. Three against three. The odds were even. So why did he feel so anxious inside?

'Let the other two go,' Salom ordered. And with that Torry and Doc released them and they began running, up the pier, past Glory and Kevin, as if they weren't there.

'The Rebels aren't very loyal,' Glory said, disgusted. 'They might have stayed and helped him.'

Now, only MacAfee stood on the pier with Torry and Doc crowded threateningly around him.

'Can't we stay and watch?' Glory pleaded. She could see Kevin was reluctant to go.

That moved him. He dragged her on. '*No!* We cannot.'

What had Salom in mind for MacAfee? Nothing bad. Nothing vicious. No. Not Salom. Yet somewhere deep inside, alarm bells were ringing. He felt something was going to happen, and he wasn't going to be there when it did.

Glory, danger over, began to talk nervously, quickly, nipping annoyingly into his train of thought.

'Are you listening, Kev?' she asked.

'No,' he said honestly, hoping she would shut up.

She didn't. 'I said, I think Salom likes me.' She waited for confirmation of this, for her brother to tell her she was all Salom ever talked about. When he said nothing, she continued brightly, 'I'm sure he does. I mean, he just saved my life.'

Kevin sniggered. 'I don't really think your life was in danger. You were only tied to a lamp post.'

But being untied from a lamp post was not half as romantic as having your life saved. Glory sighed. 'Do you think I should send him a thank-you card?'

Kevin burst out laughing. Glory was priceless.

'I don't see what's so funny!' she said, puzzled. And she strode on ahead in a huff.

In an instant, Kevin's thoughts were back to what was happening on the pier.

He followed Glory on to the brightly lit streets. It was still early and people were coming and going. No one was aware of the drama that was unfolding just a few metres away from them. A long line of people, who had just emerged from the nearby bingo hall, were waiting at a bus stop. Here, he was sure, Glory would be safe. He had to go back. He just had to.

'Now you stay here. Keep our place,' he told her. 'I have to go to the toilet.' He knew that if he told her he was going back, she would insist on coming.

'But there aren't any toilets near here,' Glory said.

'I know.' He pointed to one of the Portakabins along the road. 'I'll go behind there.'

Glory's mouth curled in disgust. 'Ooo! You are disgusting, Kevin Davidson.'

She turned away from him and Kevin ran, past the Portakabins and back down towards the pier. Running faster and faster, something deep inside telling him there was no time to waste.

He stopped dead when he heard voices drifting to him through the night air. Salom and MacAfee. One soft like silk, the other scared and shaking. It was easy to tell which was which.

From behind the old ticket office he had a full view of what was going on. It took a moment for his eyes to become accustomed to the growing dusk. When they did, he couldn't for a moment believe what he was seeing.

Salom, one push at a time, was edging MacAfee closer and closer to the river. Even in the dark, Kevin could see MacAfee's sweating, frightened face. 'B-but . . . I can't swim,' he was stuttering.

'Best way to learn then,' Torry said with delight. 'You either swim or you drown.'

Another push, and Salom's soft voice came again. 'I'll teach you to pick on any of the Tribe.'

MacAfee could hardly breathe. He sounded as if he was ready to cry. 'Please. Please, Salom. I can't swim. We wouldn't have hurt her, just had a bit of fun and let her go.'

There was no defiance in his voice now. He was too terrified; too close to the deep, dark water below the pier.

Another push. MacAfee cried out. He had stumbled against the edge. Here, there was nothing to hold on to. Nothing to break his fall. 'Salom!' MacAfee screamed his name. 'I'm sorry. I'll never do anything like that again. Please don't push me in! Please!'

He was crying now. There, in front of them all. Terrified. Humiliated.

No one . . . . *No one* had the right to frighten anybody like that. Kevin wanted to step out, to run, to save MacAfee. So why couldn't he move? Because Salom had saved his sister? Because it would look ungrateful? Because Salom was his friend?

Someone had to save MacAfee.

But it wasn't Kevin.

Suddenly, it was Doc who sprang forward. 'That's enough. Let him go!'

Salom didn't even turn his head. 'He's our enemy.'

'He's not my enemy. He's just a boy, and he can't swim. Let him go.'

Then Salom turned. 'You going to make me?' Gone was the smile that Salom always wore. Here was a face that was vicious. Scary.

Doc said slowly, 'If I have to.' With one movement he pulled MacAfee back from the edge. 'Run!' he shouted.

MacAfee stumbled, then he was racing away from them.

Kevin pressed himself against the ticket office as he passed. But MacAfee was too relieved to be free to notice anything.

Salom was still staring at Doc. 'You shouldn't have done that.'

Even Torry sounded angry. 'You shouldn't go against Salom. Not in front of MacAfee. He's our leader.'

Doc looked at him. 'Torry, MacAfee would have drowned if he'd fallen in there.'

Torry shrugged as if that didn't matter. And in that moment, Kevin thought how stupid Torry really was. Lovable and mischievous and funny, but stupid. Too much in awe of Salom to think for himself.

'You'll be sorry you did that, Doc,' Salom said, in a

tone Kevin had never heard him use before. Worse than a threat.

Salom brushed past Doc and, with Torry at his heels, he began striding up the pier.

Time for Kevin to go, unseen. Because something told him it would be better if he pretended he had seen nothing of this.

22

Glory didn't stop talking all the way home. She was excited and afraid, but there was more. Salom had saved her. To Glory, nothing else mattered. No one else had been there. Not Torry or Doc or even her brother.

'I never did believe anything I heard about him anyway,' she gabbled.

Kevin stopped. 'What did you hear about him?'

'I thought you would have known,' she said. When he shook his head, she went on. 'Well, there was this boy, years and years ago. He lived next door to Salom. But I don't believe it was Salom's fault.'

The girl was infuriating. Why could she never tell a story properly?

'What boy? And what happened?' He only just stopped himself from shouting. Shouting would only have made her stomp away and tell him nothing.

'This boy told his dad Salom was bullying him. The boy's dad was really angry, got Salom into a lot of trouble about it. Then the boy fell down a flight of stairs at the flats. He said someone had pushed him, but he hadn't seen who it was. Everyone suspected Salom. They said he had the "evil eye".'

The 'evil eye'. The words chilled Kevin. Hadn't those been the exact words one of the neighbours had used to describe Salom?

'And he still can't walk properly.' Glory broke into his thoughts.

'What?'

'This boy, he ended up with a limp,' she said. And she added with an assurance that could only come from someone with a crush, 'It was a terrible shame, but nothing to do with Salom.'

Kevin walked the rest of the way home in silence. He had a lot to think about. Glory never stopped talking. Kevin just didn't listen. Not until they reached their door, that is.

'Wait till I tell Mum and Dad!' she said, excited.

'You can't tell them!' he snapped back at her. How could even Glory be so stupid? She was late home as it was. They were both bound to get into more trouble with Mum and Dad anyway. She knew how they worried about her, how much they disapproved of the gangs. And Dad would especially disapprove of any idea of revenge. Kevin could hear him now: 'The best revenge is to live a good life.'

Dad would never understand that just wasn't

enough for boys. It wasn't the way the gangs thought, the way the Tribe saw things.

'We keep our mouths shut about everything that happened tonight.' It was an order. And Glory wasn't good at obeying orders. 'If you say a word, you can forget your night with the Tribe. Right?'

It worked. When they went in, Glory never said a word.

It wasn't too hard. There was an atmosphere in the house that had never been there before. Lately, there hadn't been a lot of talking anyway.

Salom came to the house next day, just as they were clearing up after lunch.

Thankfully, Dad had just left. Kevin was sure he would have said something to Salom. It occurred to him that Salom probably thought that too. It was lucky that Salom had just missed him. Or was it more than luck? Had Salom been watching, waiting for Dad's departure before he came in? Did he really think Salom was so devious?

Mrs Davidson welcomed him, but not as warmly as before. 'Come in.' Then she called into the kitchen, 'Kevin, Salom's here.'

Glory was in the hallway faster than a speeding bullet, a stupid grin all over her face. 'I never got a chance to thank you, last night,' she said.

Her mother looked puzzled. 'Thank him. Thank him for what?'

Without hesitation Salom answered. 'Me and Kevin

are going to teach her to Rollerblade, if that's OK with you?'

Mrs Davidson smiled. Salom could still charm her.

'Just watch her. She's got two left feet. She'll never make a line dancer,' she said and gave a quick little step into the living room.

Salom laughed as he watched her go.

'Your mum's magic, Kevin,' he said.

Glory sighed. 'You're brilliant at telling lies, Salom,' she said without a blush.

'I think she meant that as a compliment,' Kevin told him.

Salom was Salom again today. The ready smile, the laughter. Kevin began to think he might have imagined last night and the vicious way Salom had spoken to Doc.

They didn't even mention the night before until they were alone and in Kevin's room. They had got rid of a grateful Glory by asking her to bring them some Coke and crisps. Glory would normally have told Kevin to dream on, that she was nobody's servant, but then that was before she fell in love.

It was Kevin who brought the subject up. He swallowed and then he said, 'So, what did you do to MacAfee?'

Salom shrugged. 'Nothing much. Gave him a little scare, that was all.'

A little scare! He called threatening to let him drown a 'little scare'?

He couldn't let it drop there. 'What do you mean?'

Salom began looking through Kevin's books on the shelf. 'We pushed him around a bit, teased him. I offered to have a fair fight with him. One against one.'

Well, thought Kevin, maybe that was true. Before he came back on the scene anything could have happened.

'But you know MacAfee,' Salom went on. 'He's a coward.'

'And that was all?'

Salom misunderstood. He grinned. 'Not enough revenge for your sister, eh? Sorry, Kev, that's as far as it went.' Then he hesitated.

'No it wasn't . . .' Kev said, wanting him to tell the truth.

Salom nodded. 'You're right, Kev. There was more. I just didn't want to tell you.'

Kevin held his breath.

'Doc wanted to go further, but I wouldn't let him. You know Doc, he can be pretty vicious. He wanted to push MacAfee in the water. But I knew MacAfee couldn't swim. So . . . I had to stop him. I knew you would have too if you'd been there.'

Kevin looked straight into Salom's smiling eyes. Couldn't he read Kevin's thoughts? See what he was thinking? You *are* brilliant at telling lies, Salom, he thought. Because, if he hadn't been there, seen everything, he would have believed every word.

Salom put a finger to his lips. 'Not a word to Doc about this. We're the Tribe. We stick together, remember?'

23

Salom had lied to him. He had told him a barefaced lie. Not knowing that Kevin had seen everything, he had thought it safe to tell him it had been Doc who'd wanted to push MacAfee into the river.

Kevin remembered clearly the cold viciousness in Salom's voice as he edged MacAfee towards the water. It hadn't sounded like the Salom he knew, the Salom he had grown to like so much.

Which one was the real Salom?

Kevin couldn't stop thinking about it. He was mixed up and confused. He hadn't liked what the Rebels had done to Glory, but it had happened because he was one of the Tribe. He certainly hadn't liked what had happened afterwards. He shivered every time he imagined what might have been if Doc hadn't been there.

MacAfee stumbling over the edge of the pier, his arms flailing as he reached out to grab something to save himself. Splashing into the murky depths, desperately trying to stay afloat, swallowing water, going under. While Salom looked down, smiling.

Would he, Kevin, have had the courage to run forward and save him? He hadn't been able to move that night. Why? Because they had saved his sister? Because Salom was his friend?

All through Monday morning's classes Kevin was caught in a dream.

'You are not paying attention, Kevin!' Mr Brechin, the maths teacher, yelled at him. 'But then, you hardly ever pay attention these days.' He said it with disappointment. Kevin, the boy he could always rely on, had let him down. Since he had joined the Tribe, there were more exciting things to do than studying maths.

'Is Glory OK?' Tommy asked him as they filed out of the class.

Tommy, his best friend, and he'd deserted him. Tommy, who had raced to warn him about Glory and had then been sent packing because he wasn't needed any more.

Kevin felt his face go red. He was suddenly ashamed. 'Sh-she's fine. We got her.' He stammered the words out.

'I bet you felt like punching lumps out of MacAfee,' Tommy said.

Kevin wanted to tell him everything then – about Doc, about Salom, about how he was feeling. He needed to tell somebody. But he couldn't. Not yet. This was Tribe business and he had to sort it out with them first.

Tommy noticed Kevin's withdrawal from him and thought he knew the reason. His smile faded. 'None of my business, of course.' He snapped the words out. Then he was off, running towards his other friends. Better friends than Kevin.

Kevin wanted to call him back. But he couldn't. Not until he had talked to Doc.

He was certain he would find him in the mall, but it was Torry he saw first, just outside the burger bar.

'Hi, Kev!' he called. 'How's Glory?'

'In her glory,' Kev told him with disgust.

Torry found that amusing. 'Fancies our great leader even more now, eh?'

Our great leader. Kevin suddenly didn't like those words. He had never wanted anyone to be his leader. What had changed him? 'Maybe it's about time we had another election. Get a new leader?'

Torry was even more amused. 'What election? We've never had an election. Salom's always been the leader. He started the Tribe. He should be the top man. Always!'

So there were no elections, never had been. Here was another lie Salom had told him. And how many more?

'Want a bite?' Torry held out his burger to Kevin. He took one look at the mustard and tomato sauce oozing from the bun and declined.

'No thanks, I can get food poisoning just as easily at home.'

'Great night last night, wasn't it?' Torry munched.

'Yeah, sorry I didn't get a chance to punch MacAfee. You made him sorry, I bet.' He wanted to hear the truth from Torry.

'Sure did. He'll not tangle with us again.'

Kevin took a deep breath, hoping Salom hadn't already spoken to Torry.

'What exactly did you do?'

'Salom hassled him a bit, pushing him around, you know.' He began jumping about, pushing Kevin with his hand just the way he had watched Salom push MacAfee. He even mimicked Salom's voice. '"You're going to be sorry. I'm going to make you pay."' Torry laughed. 'You should have seen MacAfee's face. There'll be skid marks all over his underpants after last night.'

He munched into his burger.

'And . . . that was all?' Kevin tried to sound disappointed.

Torry eyed him over the bun. 'Might not have been . . . if it hadn't been for . . .'

Kevin waited for the truth. It didn't come.

'If it hadn't been for Salom. Doc wanted to push MacAfee in the water. Can you believe that? Lucky Salom was there, or goodness knows what might have happened.'

Kevin wanted to scream at him, 'That's a lie! Why are you lying, Torry?'

But he knew why. Torry would do anything for Salom. Salom was his hero. He probably half-believed the story now anyway. No point in talking to Torry. It was Doc he had to talk to.

He glanced around the mall. 'Doc here? I was hoping to catch him.'

Torry popped the last bit of burger into his mouth.

Casually, he wiped his hands on his jacket. 'Have you not heard?' he said at last. 'Doc's in hospital. Fell down some stairs over at his place. Broke his leg.'

24

*D*oc in hospital!
Kevin raced home in a cold sweat. 'Don't get on the wrong side of Salom,' someone had once told him. Doc had. He'd gone against him in front of MacAfee, and now Doc was lying in hospital with a broken leg.

Was that his punishment?

No! Salom could never be that bad. Kevin would never believe that. Not to one of the Tribe.

He could hardly eat his dinner for thinking about it.

'Kevin? Have you lost your appetite?' his mother asked him as she lifted away his almost-untouched plate.

'Sorry, Mum,' he said. 'Would it be all right if I went to the hospital to see Doc?'

'Would it make any difference if I said no?' She watched as Kevin lowered his eyes. She sighed. 'Oh go on, but straight back.'

'I don't like that Doc,' Glory said. 'I've never seen him smile.'

'You grin enough for both of you!' Kevin said sharply, getting up from the table.

'You don't like him either. Why are you visiting him?' She answered that one herself. 'Of course, he's one of the Tribe. You always stand by each other.' She said it with pride, as if it were a wonderful thing.

Doc's family were all gathered round his bed, his mother fussing with his pillows, his old granny sitting beside him, getting stuck into all his black grapes. Two young boys, obviously Doc's younger brothers, they looked so much like him, were fighting over who should write their name on Doc's plaster first.

'Get away from there, you two!' Doc's mother yelled, and walloped the boys with Doc's comic.

Doc looked embarrassed, just as Kevin would have done. This was Doc's family, so much like Kevin's own.

'Here's one of your little friends, son.' His granny spluttered grapes all over Doc's clean sheets.

Doc looked even more embarrassed when he spotted Kevin.

Kevin smiled and hoped he didn't look too stupid. 'I just thought I'd pop in and see how you were.'

Doc shrugged his shoulders. 'I'm getting out in a few days. Just broke my leg.'

'You could have broken your neck, boy!' his granny told him, stuffing even more black grapes into her mouth. Kevin hoped they were seedless. Mind you, if she choked she was certainly in the right place for some first aid.

'How did it happen?' Kevin asked.

Doc looked at him. 'I just tripped,' he said.

'You just tripped. It was an accident?' Kevin had never felt so relieved in his life. He beamed a big smile at Doc. Doc didn't smile back.

'Why? Did you think somebody pushed me?'

Doc knew what he was thinking, Kevin was sure of it. The bell rang just then for the end of visiting.

'Hang about, Kev,' Doc said, as his mother fussed over him and his granny attempted a kiss. 'We can have a word, eh?'

Doc's mother planted a crimson kiss on his cheek. 'Boy talk, eh?' She gathered up her family like a mother hen. Granny stuffed the last of the grapes into her mouth before attempting another kiss on Doc's cheek. This time she managed it and left a residue of grape skins on his face. It looked disgusting.

'I'll bring more tomorrow, son,' she said, and she grabbed one of the boys by the scruff of the neck as he was about to slide down the ward.

Kevin took a seat beside the bed. Doc gestured after them. 'Embarrassing or what?'

'Tell me about it!' Kevin said. 'Remember, I've got El Diablo and Honey Sue.'

For a second they smiled at each other. It was the closest he had ever felt to Doc.

'Why did you come here?' Doc said. 'No one else has.'

And why hadn't they come? Kevin wondered. Wasn't that what the Tribe were supposed to be about? To be there when you needed them? Or had Salom warned them all not to?

'I saw what happened the other night. At the pier. You saved MacAfee.'

Doc wiped away his granny's kiss with the edge of the sheet. Boy, would the nurses be mad about that! 'I couldn't let him push MacAfee in. He can't swim.'

'If I'd had the courage, I would have done the same thing.' Doc had surprised him. The one in the Tribe Kevin liked least had done the thing he admired most. 'But Salom lied,' Kevin went on. 'He said it was you who wanted to push him in.'

There was almost a smile on Doc's face. 'Does that surprise you? You've got a lot to learn about Salom.'

'I heard him say you'd be sorry. And then when Torry told me about this . . .' He gestured at his broken leg.

'You thought it was Salom's revenge?' Doc bit his lip, thinking about what to say. 'I don't know, Kev. I can't be sure. It was dark on the stairs. I don't know what I tripped over, but when I fell I heard footsteps running away.'

Kevin gasped. 'Salom?'

'How would I know? No one ever knows with Salom.'

'But you do think it was him?' Kevin said.

Doc said nothing, and that was answer enough.

'What about Stash?' Kevin asked.

Doc leaned back on his pillows. 'Stash wanted out of the Tribe.'

Kevin didn't understand. 'So?'

Doc stared at him. 'Getting out of the Tribe is just as hard as getting in, Kev. That's why I'm still a member. If you want out of the Tribe, you have to do the Walk of Death again.'

Kevin thought about it. Would he have the courage to do it again? Never. He could never face that again. Suddenly he couldn't understand why he'd ever done it in the first place. He must have been mad. It was as if he was awakening from some strange dream, some nightmare, in which he'd lived in a world he had never imagined.

Yet he still had a need to defend Salom. 'But Salom said he wasn't there when Stash fell . . .'

'And Salom said I had pushed MacAfee,' Doc reminded him.

Lies, all lies. How many more had Salom told him with that engaging smile no one could resist?

'Who ever decided the Walk of Death would be the initiation test?' Kevin asked.

Yet he knew the answer to that already. Salom.

'He can be a great friend, Kev,' Doc said, 'but don't get on the wrong side of Salom. There's a dark side to Salom. A really scary side.'

Kevin stood up with determination. 'I'm going to see him, Doc. I'm going to tell him I want out of the Tribe. And I have no intention of doing the Walk of Death again.'

25

*K*evin felt as if he was waking from a long sleep.
He decided he would waste no time. He would
go to see Salom tonight.

It was Salom's mother who opened the door. Pretty
as ever, her hair piled expertly on top of her head as if
she'd just come from the hairdresser.

'Kevin! You've come to see Salom?' She was
delighted, as if it was strange for friends to pop in to
see her son. 'Salom!' she called as she led Kevin inside
their flower-scented flat.

Salom appeared from his bedroom. 'What brings
you here?' he asked.

'I went to the hospital to see Doc. I thought I might
have seen you there.' He watched for Salom's reaction.

He didn't bat an eyelid. 'I thought it was only
family who were allowed to visit.' He smiled. 'What
happened to him anyway?'

Kevin hesitated before he answered. 'Doc thinks
someone might have tripped him.'

Again no reaction. And once again Kevin had
doubts. Surely he must be wrong. Salom looked so
blameless. 'Did he see who?'

'He only heard footsteps running away,' Kevin
admitted.

'When we find out who it was, we'll get them,' Salom said. It couldn't have been Salom, Kevin thought. Not if he was talking like this. Kevin knew, more than anything, that he didn't want it to be Salom.

Kevin sat down on Salom's bed. 'That's all we ever seem to do. They do something to us, we do something back. It's silly.'

Salom swung round in his chair. 'It's revenge.'

The best revenge is to live a good life. Again he heard his dad's words. He'd always thought his dad talked rubbish with his little sayings. Now it seemed the most sensible thing he had ever heard. 'I don't want to do it any more,' he said.

Salom swung round again, his eyes not meeting Kevin's. 'What do you mean?'

But he knew exactly what Kevin meant. He just wanted him to say it.

Kevin took a deep breath. 'I don't want to be in the Tribe any more.'

Still Salom didn't look up at him. 'You can't do that, Kevin. Once you're in the Tribe, you're always in the Tribe. Remember the oath?'

'It's a gang, Salom, not a religion.'

'We've had fun, haven't we?'

Yes, he had to admit they had had fun. But with the fun, there were the fights. There was his sister caught up in it. It wasn't worth it.

'Is that the only reason?' Salom asked him.

'No.' He decided to have this out with Salom. 'You lied to me. You said you saved MacAfee –'

Before he could continue, Salom interrupted. 'And Doc told you different. So, you believe Doc? Ask Torry what happened.'

'I already have. Torry backs you up. He always would. That's not a real friend, Salom. Remember, you said I was your best friend. Your best friend can tell you the truth. But you haven't told me the truth. You see, I saw everything, Salom. Heard everything. I was there. Hiding. Watching.'

For a split second Salom's eyes flashed with anger. He'd been found out, and he wasn't used to that. 'So what? I was helping Glory.'

Kevin shook his head. 'No, Salom. You were frightening somebody. You humiliated MacAfee, and you enjoyed it. I don't want to be a part of that any more.'

Salom sat up straight in the chair. He was getting angry, Kevin was sure of that. 'So you think you can leave, just like that. Well, you can, but only if you do the Walk of Death again.'

Kevin had been waiting for this. He was ready. 'Stuff the Walk of Death!' he said. 'I'm finished with that rubbish. I was a twit to do it before. There is no way I'll do it again. Never!'

Salom was on the edge of his seat. 'You think I'm going to let you walk away from the Tribe?'

Kevin laughed. 'I'll do anything I want to do. I don't take orders from anybody.'

Kevin knew they were shouting. Any minute now he expected Salom's mother to rush in through the door to protect her boy.

Salom sneered at him. 'I can make you really sorry you said that.'

'Like you made Doc sorry? Gonna push me down some stairs too? Can't you ever do anything to someone's face?'

Suddenly, Salom leapt at him. Kevin fell back off the bed and they both rolled on to the floor, punching wildly at each other's face. Salom's fist landed hard on Kevin's eye, but a punch of Kevin's hit Salom squarely on the jaw. Kevin jumped to his feet and hurled himself at Salom. They both fell against the door. Salom grabbed Kevin's head and banged it against the woodwork. Kevin let out a yell of pain, then he was on Salom again, his fist raised ready to punch hard into him.

And then suddenly Salom's mother burst into the room, screaming. 'What's going on here?' She pulled them apart and pushed Kevin away from her son roughly. 'Get out of this house!' she yelled. Then she turned all her attention on Salom. 'Are you all right? Let me see that jaw!'

Salom pulled away from her, but all the time his eyes never left Kevin. There was real venom in that look. 'You'll be sorry,' he mouthed.

Kevin backed out. He didn't trust Salom with his back turned. Come to that, he didn't trust Salom's mother.

'Is that another friend turned against him?' Kevin backed right into Salom's father. He spat out the words, holding Kevin by the shoulders. 'It was his fault, wasn't it? It's always his fault.' His voice was low and calm and he was looking at Salom as if he hated him.

But Salom's venomous gaze never left Kevin.

Salom's mother leapt at her husband. 'What would you know? You're never sober. You don't care what he does.' She was screaming now, pushing her son behind her protectively.

'I should have got my belt to him long ago.' There was more anger in that flat, calm voice than in all Salom's mother's screaming.

'Over my dead body. You'll never lay a hand on that boy!'

Kevin backed away. They didn't even notice him going. They were too wrapped up in their own hatred. He ran for the door. He wanted out of this house, away from this madhouse. He wanted back to the sanity that was Glory, and El Diablo and Honey Sue.

26

*I*t was a strange feeling that would take a bit of getting used to, not being one of the Tribe.

He was his own person again. He could go where he wanted. Do what he wanted. He liked that. He felt free.

At school next day, he paid attention at all his classes, even laughed with some of his classmates when Mr Bennetti, the science teacher, tried to insult him with one of his rotten jokes. 'The last time I saw a face like yours, Davidson, I threw it a banana.'

He wouldn't have laughed when he was one of the Tribe. He would have been too cool to laugh then. Now, he felt normal again. It was over, and he was glad. At break time he spoke to Tommy, though Tommy hardly spoke back to him. Kevin couldn't blame him for that. He hadn't been much of a friend to Tommy. But he wouldn't give up.

He saw him again at lunchtime and asked him nervously if he'd like to come over to his house that night. 'I've got this great game, Tommy. You'll love it.' He realized how afraid he was that Tommy might say no.

Tommy hesitated. 'Who else is coming?'

'Just you and me, Tommy. Honest.'

'I've got band practice after school,' Tommy said. Was he looking for an excuse not to come? Kevin couldn't tell.

'So has Glory. You could come home together.'

Tommy curled his lip. 'With Glory? Are you kidding? You know it takes her ages to walk home. She talks to everybody.'

Kevin smiled. If Tommy came tonight, it would be just like old times.

When he told his mother that Tommy was coming, she was delighted. 'I hope that you and Tommy are going to be friends again,' she said. 'I miss him coming round.'

'And what about Salom?' Kevin asked her.

His mother sighed. 'Salom is one of those boys you take to right away, and then . . .' She thought about it. 'And then you begin to have all sorts of doubts about him.'

All sorts of doubts. Yes. That was exactly it with Salom.

Tonight was their line dancing, so immediately after tea Mum and Dad turned into El Diablo and Honey Sue and went off for an evening of country and western heaven.

'Remember to tell Glory I've left her macaroni cheese just to be heated in the microwave,' Honey Sue reminded him before she left. 'And there's crisps and juice for you and Tommy.'

He watched them from the window and thought how lucky he was. His mum and dad were daft as brushes and could be mega embarrassing at times, but he always felt safe with them. He knew they loved him.

Doc's family were like his, warm and loving. They probably worried about him too. Not like Torry's. He remembered Torry telling him he could do what he wanted, they didn't care. Poor Torry. No wonder he needed the Tribe so much. And Salom too. To be a pawn between a father who didn't love him at all and a mother who smothered him with too much love. Salom needed the Tribe too. The Tribe were his family. A family who looked up to him. The only real family he had.

It had begun to rain when Tommy arrived. He shook out his anorak on the landing.

'Hungry?' Kevin asked.

'Starving.'

'We'll eat Glory's macaroni cheese. Let's get her really mad.'

He led him into the kitchen. 'She'll not be needing it tonight anyway,' Tommy said, helping himself to juice from the fridge. Just like he used to in the old days.

Kevin waited till they were eating before he told him. 'I'm finished with the Tribe, Tommy,' he said.

Tommy looked puzzled. 'I thought you were just having a night off because . . .' He shrugged. 'Why?'

'It was exciting for a while,' Kevin admitted. 'But it's all chasing and fighting, and it's silly. I was born for a quieter life.'

'I'm glad, Kev,' Tommy said. 'I don't like that Salom. I could never understand why you liked him so much.'

How could he explain? Tommy would never understand. 'By the way, what did you mean: Glory won't be needing her macaroni cheese?' he asked casually. Glory could eat macaroni cheese during her sleep.

'They were going into the chip shop when I saw them,' Tommy said. 'That's why I thought you were having a night off.'

Warning bells, faint but getting louder with every second, were beginning to sound.

'They? Who're they?'

Tommy saw the worry in Kevin's face and he began to worry too. 'I thought you knew. That's why I never mentioned it.'

'Who're they, Tommy?' He was really worried now.

'Salom,' Tommy said. 'Salom and Glory. Kevin, you've gone chalk white.'

He felt as if the blood had drained from him. What a fool he'd been to think it was over. What a fool!

'I'll make you sorry,' Salom had warned him. And now Glory was with him. But why? What was the worst thing he could do to Glory?

And in that split second he knew the answer.

Glory wanted to be one of the Tribe. And tonight, Salom would invite her to join.

All she had to do . . . was the Walk of Death.

27

'You can't be serious! Even Salom wouldn't make her do that!'

He'd told Tommy about the Walk of Death, broken the oath of silence in the seconds after he'd realized what Salom must have in mind.

'I have a gut feeling I'm right, Tommy. I told him I'd never do it again. And this is how he's getting back at me. He'll make Glory do it.'

Tommy still looked disbelieving. But he didn't know Salom. Didn't understand how his mind worked.

'We've got to get there, Tommy.'

'We?' Tommy asked, so used now to being left out.

But Kevin didn't wait for an answer. He was already hauling on his jacket and making for the door.

The old whisky warehouse was on the other side of town. Miles away.

'We'll wait for ages for a bus,' Kevin said, agitated and frightened. Frightened for Glory.

'We'll get a taxi then.' Tommy pulled a five-pound note from his pocket. 'Got paid for my paper round today.' Good old Tommy! What had Kevin ever done without him?

'That's a dangerous place to go at night, boys,' the taxi driver warned them as he dropped them at the end of the street. 'Sure you'll be all right?'

'No bother, mister,' Kevin shouted, and they began to run up the unlit road.

'Maybe you're wrong, Kevin,' Tommy said breathlessly. 'Maybe right now Glory's screaming blue murder because we've finished her macaroni.'

Kevin knew he wasn't wrong. This was Salom's perfect revenge.

They were almost there, making for the gaping, broken doorway, when suddenly, out of nowhere, stepped MacAfee. Behind him, one by one, the Rebels emerged from darkened doorways.

MacAfee spat at him, Kevin dodged back. MacAfee looked at Tommy and spat again. 'Has he joined the Tribe now?' He sneered and then called back to his gang, 'Hey, boys, they must be getting desperate.'

Kevin had no time for this. 'Let us past, MacAfee! Get out of our way!' He screamed the words out, trying to run past him.

MacAfee and two of the Rebels barred their way. 'You want to make us?'

Kevin could see it was no use. MacAfee and the Rebels were itching for a fight, for revenge. It was all so stupid. Why had it taken him so long to realize that?

'We followed Salom here. Him and your sister.'

Kevin gasped. He'd been right. Salom had Glory.

'But we lost them,' MacAfee went on. 'So if we can't get him, you'll do just as well.'

It was time, Kevin thought, to let Macafee have his revenge.

'You really want Salom?' Kevin asked. MacAfee said nothing. 'Of course you do. Remember what he was going to do to you at the pier?'

He could see the shock in MacAfee's eyes. He had not realized that Kevin had seen it all, witnessed his humiliation. 'Do you remember how he made you feel, MacAfee? Salom's got my sister up there.' He nodded towards the old warehouse. 'I don't want him to make my sister feel like that.'

MacAfee moved restlessly, thinking it over. Taking too long.

'You always wanted to know what the initiation test for the Tribe was?' Now all at once he had MacAfee's full attention. 'Well, follow me. I'm going to show you what it is.'

MacAfee hesitated. 'Is this a trap?' he said.

Kevin shook his head. 'Not this time, promise. Just follow me!'

And then he ran, past MacAfee, past them all. He heard MacAfee rallying the other Rebels.

'Come on!'

And then they were all running, racing towards the old dark warehouse and the broken stairs that led up to the Walk of Death.

28

*T*he steps were damp and slippery and the darkness intense. Could he remember what floor it was on? The Rebels raced up the steps behind him, two at a time, eager to know the secret, not to help Glory. Kevin didn't care. They were there.

One more floor. Would he ever reach it? Maybe he was wrong. He hoped and prayed he was wrong. Salom liked Glory. Sometimes he seemed to be as fond of her as if she'd been his own sister. Surely he wouldn't risk her life on the Walk of Death?

And yet . . .

There was a dark side to Salom. A side Kevin could never understand. If someone went against him, he needed revenge.

He turned on one more floor. Suddenly, a blast of wind and rain caught his face and he knew he was there. He held Tommy back by the arm. Placed a finger to his lips. He couldn't risk a noise now, not if Glory was balanced somewhere between life and death.

He swung round one of the old pillars, and there was what he had dreaded seeing: Glory, halfway along the Walk of Death. He caught his breath. Salom was standing on the other side, encouraging her to come on. He was smiling, but there was something about that smile that scared the life out of Kevin.

'You can do it, Glory. You're brilliant,' he was saying softly.

Tommy saw them in the same instant and couldn't keep quiet. 'Glory!' he called out in alarm.

Taken by surprise, Glory turned her head. She began to rock, her balance going. *No!* She mustn't fall.

Kevin ran forward. 'Stand up straight, Glory!' he ordered.

Her voice was shaking when she answered. 'I-I-I can't. I'm too scared.'

'Come on, Glory. If I can do it, so can you. You're better than any boy, remember?'

Glory was biting her lip, trying not to cry. Her eyes went down. The last thing he wanted her to do. 'No!' His voice was still soft, but firm. He tried to remember how he had felt as he walked across. Just the way Glory was feeling now.

A rush of footsteps behind him. The Rebels were here.

Salom's eyes filled with venom when he saw them. 'What are they doing here?' His menacing gaze moved to Kevin. 'You betrayed us.'

'Yes, I did.' Kevin said it proudly. 'This, MacAfee, is the Walk of Death.'

He could hear their gasps as the Rebels realized what it entailed. They hadn't expected anything as life-threatening as this. None of them would have been brave enough or stupid enough to do it.

'Kev, help me.' Glory's voice was soft but filled with terror.

'Come to me, Glory.' Salom coaxed her. And Kevin was sure that was the worst thing she could do. She had to come back to him. Yet how could she? Coming back would be even more dangerous than going on. It would mean turning around. But going on would lead her straight to Salom.

No. That would be the most dangerous thing of all.

There was only one thing for it. He was mad to even consider it, but it had to be done. 'I'm coming to get you, Glory,' he whispered.

Tommy grabbed his arm. 'No, Kev. That beam might not hold both of you. It's too dangerous.'

He could hear Glory's panting breath. 'Kev.' She spoke his name like a prayer.

And he knew then he had no choice. He had to bring her back.

'Better you than me, pal,' MacAfee said.

This time Kevin didn't hesitate. He looked at Glory standing, terrified, in the middle of the beam and he began to walk across. He wouldn't look down, he would forget the black depth beneath him. He would concentrate only on Glory.

'When I get close, Glory,' he said taking another faltering step, 'I'm going to sit astride the beam. Then I'll help you to sit down too and we'll bum our way back. OK?'

He could hear her breathing, quick and heavy.

'She'd be safer coming on to me,' Salom said softly.

'No, she wouldn't.' Kevin looked straight at Salom, standing at the other end of the beam. 'No, she wouldn't. I don't trust you, Salom.'

'Go on, Kev. You're almost there.' Tommy's voice was behind him, urging him on. A voice to be trusted. Not as exciting as Salom's, but a voice that would never let him down.

He was so close now, he could touch Glory. But he didn't dare. He could see her shaking with fear. But Glory still stood straight.

'I'm going to sit on the beam, Glory,' he said. It was trickier than he had thought. More dangerous. Nothing to hold on to as he bent and crouched down. A wave of nausea hit him as he caught a glimpse of what was below. Nothing. An eternity of empty floors. *No!*

He drew his eyes away, concentrated on gripping

the beam with both hands and letting first one leg swing over and then the other. He had made it. Now at least he was sitting. He edged closer to Glory, murmuring words of comfort all the time. He gripped one of her legs and it shook under his hand. She's going to pull us both down, he thought, as terrified as she was.

'I want you to crouch down, Glory. You're OK. I've got you.'

She tried to move, still shaking.

'Steady now,' Kevin whispered. 'You can do it. Just pretend you're on the beam at school.'

There was no sound around them, only the wind and rain outside. It was as if the Rebels and Tommy had disappeared, they were so silent.

Kevin could feel Salom's eyes boring into him. But he wouldn't look. All his concentration was on Glory.

Glory was crouching now. He could hear the sob in her voice when she spoke. 'Oh, Kev. Oh, Kev . . .' She kept repeating his name, like a litany. 'If I survive, I'll never do anything this silly again.'

'That would take a miracle,' he told her. And in that instant she was down in front of him. A cheer went up from Tommy and the Rebels. But from Salom only silence.

'Now, we have to bum our way back.'

Glory tutted. 'Please don't use the B-word, Kev,' she said nervously. He squeezed her shoulders. Their lives were literally hanging in the balance, and yet she was telling him off for saying 'bum'!

They began edging their way back slowly. He held

her by the waist. He could feel that she was more relaxed now. 'We're going to get splinters in our . . .' She giggled with nerves.

'I can live with that,' Kevin whispered in her ear.

They were going to make it. He felt his own body relax. They were going to make it.

Then it happened.

An ominous creak.

'What was that?' Glory stammered.

Before Kevin could answer, Tommy shouted, 'Get back here, quick. The beam's going to go!'

Another creak. Kevin felt movement beneath him. Glory screamed. Now it really was a race against time.

Only a short distance to go. Yet if this beam went, it would be far too far.

'Come on, Kev! Give me your hand.' Tommy held out his hand. Kevin could almost reach him. He slipped his arm tighter round Glory's waist. The beam was going. It moved beneath him. It creaked, it crackled. No time to waste. He grabbed Tommy's hand, just reaching it. One pull and they would be safe. But one more creak and the beam would rend itself apart and tumble down. He couldn't wait any longer. He threw himself back, dragging Glory with him. MacAfee reached down and grabbed a screaming Glory by the hair, by the collar. Tommy grabbed Kevin's jacket and pulled. MacAfee dragged at Glory.

The beam gave way, splintered and broke in two just as Kevin and his sister were hauled to safety.

They watched as it tumbled, crashing its way down

the murky floors below. It sent up clouds of dust and debris as it fell. They seemed to be watching for ever, mesmerized, until at last it crashed to the ground far beneath them.

The Walk of Death was no more.

'I thought he liked me, Kev,' Glory sobbed. 'I thought Salom really liked me.'

Kevin gazed across the chasm into the gloom at the other side, and caught his breath.

Salom had gone.

29

*K*evin never saw Salom again. No one did. Within the next few days, Salom and his mother left the district.

'And about time too!' some said, glad to be rid of him. 'That mother of his has a lot to answer for.'

Yet others blamed his father. 'He's a drunk. Always been a drunk. He never gave the boy a chance. I'll never understand why she stayed with him so long.'

Who was right? And which was the real Salom? The friend whose voice held so much sadness when he said, 'You don't know how lucky you are to have a normal family', or the boy who had the wickedness in him to use Glory – smiling, adoring Glory – to get his revenge?

Perhaps he'd never know. Never find out.

There were mysteries still surrounding Salom. What did happen to Stash? Who pushed Doc? Questions that might never be answered.

Without Salom there was no Tribe, and without the Tribe the other gangs lost their fascination. No one had ever beaten the Tribe, and now no one ever could.

As for Glory, she recovered miraculously. Kevin even had a horrible notion that she had turned her attention on MacAfee. 'He saved my life,' she kept telling him.

Would Glory never learn any sense? He hoped not. He kind of liked his daft sister just the way she was.

So, it was over. The spell had been broken and life became normal again. Or as normal as it could be if you lived with the Davidsons.

Yet sometimes, in the middle of the night, he'd still wake up sweating. Remembering the oath he had sworn in blood in that candlelit shop so long ago. Remembering the vengeance promised for anyone who broke it: 'Haunted for the rest of his life by ghosts and demons.'

And he would imagine Salom in the dark corner of the room, ready to step out of the shadows with that enigmatic smile on his face, and Kevin knew then that what he had read on that wall long ago was true . . .

SALOM IS EVIL.